Bob and Sheila Beckwith have a perfect marriage, exciting careers, and two lovely daughters. Sheila never knew that Bob had once been unfaithful—ten years ago, on a business trip to France. Bob never knew that this brief affair had produced a child.

Now the French woman is dead. And the little boy—Bob's son—has no one in the world.

What should Bob Beckwith do?

———————

"MEMORABLE . . . REMINISCENT OF THE LATE JOHN O'HARA."
Pittsburgh Press

MAN,
WOMAN
AND CHILD

Erich Segal

BALLANTINE BOOKS • NEW YORK

Library of Congress Catalog Card Number: 79-3414

ISBN 0-345-31263-5

This edition published by arrangement with
Harper & Row, Publishers

A portion of this work first appeared in *Family Circle*

Manufactured in the United States of America

First International Ballantine Books Edition: February 1981
First Printing: June 1981
Eighth Printing: April 1983

Cover photo by Anthony Loew

For my beloved Karen

A wife of valor who can find?
She is far more precious than jewels.

Proverbs 31:10

Things fall apart; the center cannot
   hold . . .
The ceremony of innocence is
   drowned . . .

—W. B. Yeats, "The Second Coming"

I HAVE AN IMPORTANT MESSAGE FOR YOU, DR. Beckwith."

"I'm tied up right now. Can I get back to you?"

"Actually, Professor, I'd prefer to speak to you in person."

An "urgent" phone call had summoned Robert Beckwith from the final departmental meeting of the term. It was the French consulate.

"Can you get to Boston before five?" the undersecretary asked.

"It's almost four-thirty now," said Bob.

"I will wait for you."

"Is it *that* important?"

"Yes, I believe so."

Totally mystified, Bob walked back across the hall to where the five other senior members of the MIT Statistics Department were waiting. Citing the unimportance of their agenda when compared to the excellence of the weather, he moved that they adjourn until the fall. As usual, there was one objection.

"I must say, Beckwith, this is rather unprofessional," huffed P. Herbert Harrison.

"Let's put it to a vote, Herb," Bob replied.

The score was five to one in favor of vacation.

Bob hurried to his car and began threading his way across the Charles River through the heavy rush hour traffic. Moving slower than the passing joggers, he had plenty of time to speculate on what could possibly be so urgent. And the more he thought, the more the odds seemed to suggest one thing: They're giving me the Legion of Honor.

It's not so impossible, he told himself. After all, I've lectured lots of times in France—twice at the Sorbonne. Hell, I even drive a Peugeot.

That must be it. I'm going to get one of those little red anchovies for my lapel. I may even have to start wearing jackets. Who cares? It'll be worth it to see the jealousy on certain faculty faces. God, Sheila and the girls will be proud.

"This message came to us by telex," said M. Bertrand Pelletier the moment Bob sat down in his elegant high-ceilinged office. He held a narrow slip of paper.

Here it comes, thought Bob. The award. He tried not to smile too soon.

"It requests that Dr. Beckwith of MIT contact a Monsieur Venarguès in Sète immediately." He handed Bob the paper.

"Sète?" repeated Bob. And thought, Oh no, it can't be.

"Charming little village, if a bit *gaucho*," said Pelletier. "Do you know the south of France?"

"Uh—yes." Bob grew even more uneasy when he noticed that the consular official wore a rather solemn expression.

"Monsieur Pelletier, what's this all about?"

"I was only informed that it concerns the late Nicole Guérin."

My God, Nicole. So long ago, so well suppressed he almost had convinced himself it never happened. The single infidelity in all his years of marriage.

Why *now*? Why after all this time? And hadn't she herself insisted they would never meet again, never contact one another?

Wait a minute.

"Monsieur Pelletier, did you say the *late* Nicole Guérin? She's dead?"

The undersecretary nodded.

"I regret that I have no details. I am sorry, Dr. Beckwith."

Did this man know any more?

"And who's this person I'm supposed to call?"

The undersecretary shrugged. Which, translated from the French, meant that he didn't know—and didn't care to.

"May I offer my *condoléances*, Dr. Beckwith?"

This, translated from the French, meant it was getting late. And M. Pelletier no doubt had plans for other things. It was, after all, a balmy evening in the month of June.

Bob took the hint. He stood up.

"Thank you, Monsieur Pelletier."

"Not at all."

They shook hands.

A bit unsteadily, Bob walked out onto Commonwealth Avenue. He was parked diagonally across, right near the Ritz. Should he get a quick shot of courage at the bar? No. Better make that phone call first. And somewhere private.

*   *   *

The entire corridor was silent. Everyone seemed to have left for the summer. Bob closed the office door, sat at his desk and dialed France.

"*Wuy?*" croaked a sleepy voice with a thick Provençal accent.

"Uh—this is Robert Beckwith. May I speak with Monsieur Venarguès?"

"Bobbie—it is me, Louis! At last I've found you. What a task. . . ."

Even after all these years, that voice was unmistakable. The rasp created by the smoke of fifty million Gauloises.

"Louis the mayor?"

"*Ex*-mayor. Can you imagine? They put me out to pasture like some ancient dinosaur. The Council—"

Bob was much too tense for lengthy anecdotes.

"Louis, what is this about Nicole?"

"Oh, Bobbie, what a tragedy. Five days ago. Head-on collision. She was coming from a cardiac emergency. The whole town is in mourning. . . ."

"Oh. I'm sorry—"

"Can you imagine? She was so young. A saint, unselfish. All the Faculty of Medicine from Montpellier came to the service. You know she hated religion, Bobbie, but we had to."

He paused to sigh. Bob seized the opportunity.

"Louis, this is terrible news. But I don't see why you wanted me to call you. I mean, it's been ten years since I last saw her."

Suddenly a silence on the line. Then Louis answered almost in a whisper: "Because of the child."

"Child? Was Nicole married?"

"No, no. Of course not. She was an 'independent mother,' so to speak. She raised the boy herself."

"But I still don't see what this has to do with me," said Bob.

"Uh—Bobbie, I do not know how to say this. . . ."

"Say it!"

"He is your child too," said Louis Venarguès.

For a moment there was silence on both sides of the Atlantic. Bob was stunned beyond speech.

"Bobbie, are you still there? *Allo?*"

"What?"

"I know you are perhaps shocked by this news."

"No, Louis. I'm not shocked. I simply don't believe it," Bob replied, as anger helped him to regain his powers of speech.

"But it's true. I was her confidant in everything."

"But what the hell makes you so sure that *I'm* the father?"

"Bobbie," Louis answered gently, "you were here in May. The demonstrations, you recall? The little boy came—so to speak—on schedule. There was no one else in her life at the time. She would have told me. Of course, she never wanted you to know."

Jesus Christ, thought Bob, this is incredible.

"Dammit, Louis, even if it's true, I'm not responsible for—"

"Bobbie, tranquilize yourself. No one's saying that you have responsibility. Jean-Claude is well provided for. Believe me—I am the executor." He paused and added, "There is only one small problem."

Bob trembled at the possibilities.

"What?" he asked.

"The boy has absolutely no one. Nicole had no other family. He's all alone."

Bob did not reply. He was still trying to gauge the direction of this conversation.

"Ordinarily, we would take him in, Marie-Thérèse and I. . . ." Louis paused. "We are his guardians. But she is ill, Bob, gravely ill. She doesn't have much time."

"I'm sorry," Bob interjected softly.

"What can I say? We had a honeymoon of forty years. But now you see why it's impossible. Unless we can find some alternative—and quickly—the authorities will take the boy away."

At last Bob sensed where this was leading. He grew angrier with every breath. And frightened.

"The child is inconsolable," Louis continued. "He is sad beyond tears. His grief is so great he cannot even cry. He just sits there—"

"Get to the point," said Bob.

Louis hesitated.

"I want to tell him."

"Tell him what?"

"That you exist."

"No! Are you crazy? How could that possibly help?"

"I just want him to know that somewhere in this world he has a father. It would be *something*, Bobbie."

"Louis, for God's sake! I'm a married man with two young daughters. Look, I'm truly sorry about Nicole. I'm sorry about the boy. But I refuse to get involved in this. I will not hurt my family. I can't. I *won't*. That's final."

There was another silence on the line. Or at least ten seconds of nonverbal static.

"All right," said Louis at last. "I'll trouble you no more. But I do confess I'm very disappointed."

Too damn bad.

"Good night, Louis."

Yet another pause (for Bob to reconsider), and then at last capitulation.

"Goodbye, Bobbie," he mumbled, and hung up.

Bob put down the receiver and buried his head in his hands. This was too difficult to take in all at once. After so many years, Nicole Guérin, back in his life. And could their brief affair really have produced a child? A son?

Oh, God, what should I do?

"Evenin', Perfesser."

Bob looked up, startled.

It was Lilah Coleman, on her daily rounds of tidying the offices.

"How are you, Mrs. Coleman?"

"Not too bad. How's yer statistics?"

"Oh, pretty good."

"Say, you ain't run across some likely numbers, have ya? Rent's due an' my luck's been pretty lousy lately."

"Sorry, Mrs. Coleman, I don't feel too lucky myself."

"Well, as they say, Perfesser, 'if you don't feel it, don't play it.' Anyway, that's my philosophy. You gotta trust your gut."

She emptied his wastebasket and whisked a cloth across his desk.

"Well, I'll be rollin' on, Perfesser. Have a good summer. An' rest that brilliant brain o' yours."

She left and softly closed the door. But something she had said stuck with him. Trust your gut. Quite unprofessional. But very human.

He sat frozen, staring at the telephone, long after Mrs. Coleman's footsteps faded down the corridor. He felt a desperate inward struggle, heart and mind at war. Don't be crazy, Bob. Don't risk your marriage. Nothing's worth it. Who knows if it's even true? Forget it.

Forget it?

An impulse he could not control made him pick up the phone. Even as he dialed he wasn't sure what he would say.

"Hello—it's me, Bob."

"Ah, good. I knew that you would reconsider."

"Listen, Louis, I need time to think. I'll call you back tomorrow."

"Good, good. He is a lovely boy. But do ring a bit earlier, eh?"

"Good night, Louis."

They hung up. Now Bob was terrified. He had placed his whole existence in jeopardy. What made him call again?

Affection for Nicole? No. All he felt for her now was enormous rage.

A little boy he'd never met?

He walked like a zombie to the parking lot. He was panicked and confused. He had to talk to someone. But in the entire world he had only one close friend, one person who really understood him.

His wife, Sheila.

2

By now Route 2 was fairly empty and he reached Lexington too quickly. He had really needed more time. To gain control of himself. Organize his thoughts. What am I going to say? How the hell am I even going to face her?

"How come you're home so late, Bob?"

Paula, his nine-year-old, was in constant training to take over as his wife.

"Departmental meeting," Bob replied, deliberately ignoring her unlicensed use of his first name.

In the kitchen Jessica Beckwith, twelve and a half going on twenty-five, was discoursing with her mother. Subject: fruits, creeps, wonks and nerds.

"Really, Mom, there's not one decent male in the whole upper school."

"What's all this?" asked Bob as he entered and kissed the two older women in his family. He was determined to act naturally.

"Jessie's lamenting the quality of the opposite sex at school—or actually the lack of it."

"Then maybe you should transfer, Jess," he said, teasing her.

"Oh, Father, you are hopelessly obtuse. All of

Massachusetts is the boonies. It's a province in search of a city."

Sheila cast an indulgent smile at Bob.

"Well, Ms. Beckwith, what is your solution?" asked Bob.

Jessie blushed. Bob had interrupted her very subtle sales pitch.

"Mom knows," said Jessica.

"Europe, Bob," said Sheila. "Your daughter wants to take a Garber teen-age tour this summer."

"But she's not actually a teen-ager yet," retorted Bob.

"Oh, Daddy, how punctilious you are," sighed Jessica. "I'm old enough to go."

"But you're also young enough to wait a year."

"Daddy, I refuse to spend another summer with my bourgeois family on tedious Cape Cod."

"Then get a job."

"I would, but I'm not old enough."

"Q.E.D., Ms. Beckwith," Bob replied with satisfaction.

"Kindly spare me all your academic double-talk, will you? What if there's a nuclear war? I could die without seeing the Louvre."

"Jessica," said Bob, enjoying this interlude from his anxieties, "I have it on good authority that there won't be a nuclear war for at least three years. Ergo, you have plenty of time to see the Louvre before we get zapped."

"Daddy, don't be ghoulish."

"Jessie, it was you who brought the subject up," said Sheila, a seasoned referee for father-daughter sparring matches.

"Oh, you people are hopeless," sighed Jessica Beckwith once again, and slouched disdainfully from the kitchen.

They were alone. Why does she have to look so beautiful tonight? thought Bob.

"I wish they'd outlaw puberty," said Sheila, going to her husband for the daily evening hug she had looked forward to since breakfast. She put her arms around him. "How come you're late? More memorable orations from the Colleague?"

"Yeah. He was in rare stupefying form."

After so many years of talking to each other, they'd evolved a kind of code. For example, Bob's department had three men, two women and a "colleague"—P. Herbert Harrison, a pompous ass with lengthy and dissenting views on everything. The Beckwiths' friends had also been given nicknames.

"The Owl and the Pussycat invited us for dinner Saturday with Carole Kupersmith."

"Alone? What happened to the Ape of Chestnut Hill?"

"He went back to his wife."

They had a marriage very much in sync. And she had flawless antennae when it came to sensing his emotions.

"Are you okay?"

"Uh—sure," said Bob. "What makes you ask?"

"You look a little pale."

"Just academic pallor. Two days on the Cape and I'll be absolutely golden."

"Still, promise me you won't do any work tonight."

"Okay," said Bob. (As if he would be able to concentrate on anything.) "Have you got any pages from the Press?"

"Nothing urgent. I'm still wading through that Russo-Chinese diplomatic thing. I tell you, for a university professor, Reinhardt's prose has more starch than a laundry."

"Honey, if all authors wrote like Churchill, you'd

be unemployed. But anyway, let's neither of us work tonight."

"Fine. What'd you have in mind?" Her green eyes were shining. His heart ached at the thought of what she would have to hear.

"I love you," he said.

"Good. But in the meanwhile set the table, huh?"

"Daddy, when you were my age, how much television could you watch?" Paula glanced at Bob seductively.

"When I was your age, there was no TV."

"Are you *that* old?"

"What your father means," said Sheila, glossing Bob's hyperbole, "was he knew that reading books was more rewarding."

"We read books in school," said Paula. "Can I watch the tube now?"

"If all your homework's done," said Sheila.

"What's on?" said Bob, dutifully taking an interest in his offsprings' cultural activities.

"*Scott and Zelda,*" Jessica replied.

"Well, that sounds vaguely educational. On PBS?"

"Oh, Daddy," Jessie said with much exasperation, "don't you know *any*thing?"

"Listen, I've read every book Scott wrote, if you don't mind."

"*Scott and Zelda* is a series," Paula said disgustedly.

"About a dog from Mars and a girl from California," Jessie added.

"Fascinating. Which is which?" said Bob.

"Oh, Daddy, even Mom knows that."

Sheila looked at him with love. We poor benighted souls, she thought. We aren't with it anymore.

"Honey, go and view with them. I'll clear the table."

"No," said Bob. "I'll clear it. You go watch Scott the Wonder Dog."

"Dad, Zelda is the dog," Paula frowned, and dashed off to the living room.

"Coming, Mom?" said Jessie.

"I wouldn't miss it for anything," said Sheila as she watched her tired husband piling up the dinner dishes. "See you later, Robert."

"Yeah."

He waited until he was sure the girls were fast asleep. Sheila was curled up on the couch with a "ridiculously filthy" Hollywood novel. Jean-Pierre Rampal was playing Vivaldi, and Bob was pretending to read *The New Republic*. The tension was unbearable.

"Want a drink, hon?"

"No, thanks," said Sheila, looking up.

"Mind if I do?"

"Since when do you have to ask permission?" She went back to her novel.

"Incredible," she murmured. "You won't *believe* how they do it in this chapter. Right in the middle of Rodeo Drive."

Oh, God, he thought, how can I do this?

"Hey—can we talk for a second?"

He was now sitting a few feet from her, an unusually tall Scotch in his hand.

"Sure. Is something wrong?"

"Well, sort of. Yes."

He lowered his head. Sheila was suddenly frightened. She put her book down and sat upright.

"Bob, you aren't sick, are you?"

No, I just feel that way, he thought. But shook his head. "Honey, I gotta talk to you about something."

Sheila Beckwith felt a sudden shortening of breath. How many of her friends had heard their husbands open conversations with preambles just like this? We have to talk. About our marriage. And from the grim expression on Bob's face, she feared that he, too, was about to say, "It isn't working anymore."

"Bob," she said with candor, "something in your voice scares me. Have I done anything?"

"No, no. It's me. I've done it."

"What?"

"Oh, Jesus, you don't know how hard this is to say."

"Please, Robert, the suspense is killing me."

Bob took a breath. He was shaking.

"Sheila, remember when you were pregnant with Paula?"

"Yes?"

"I had to fly to Europe—Montpellier—to give that paper. . . ."

"And . . . ?"

A pause.

"I had an affair." He said it as quickly as he could. Like ripping off a bandage fast, to cause less pain.

Sheila's face went ashen.

"No," she said, shaking her head violently as if to drive out what she had just heard. "This is some terrible joke." She looked at him for reassurance. "Isn't it?"

"No. It's true," he said tonelessly. "I—I'm sorry."

"Who?" she asked.

"Nobody," he replied. "Nobody special."

"*Who*, Robert?"

"Her—her name was Nicole Guérin. She was a doctor." Why does she want to hear these details? he wondered.

"And how long did it last?"

"Two, three days."

"Which—two days or three days? I want to know, dammit."

"Three days," he said.

"And three nights," she added.

"Yes," he said. "Does all this matter?"

"Everything matters," Sheila answered, and then said to herself, "Jesus."

He watched her fight to keep control. This was worse than he had even imagined. Then she looked at him and asked:

"And you kept quiet all these years?"

He nodded.

"Why didn't you ever tell me? I thought our marriage was based on total honesty. Why the hell didn't you tell me?"

"I was going to," he said weakly.

"But . . . ?"

"I—I was waiting for the right moment." He knew it sounded absurd, but it was true. He had really wanted to tell her. But not like this.

"And ten years was the right moment?" she said sardonically. "No doubt you thought it would be easier. On *whom?*"

"I—I didn't want to hurt you," he said, knowing any answer would be futile. And then he added, "Sheila, if it's any consolation, that's the only time. I swear. It was the only time."

"No," she answered softly, "it isn't consolation. Once is more than never."

She bit her lip to hold back tears. And he had more to say.

"Sheila, that was so damn long ago. I had to tell you now because—"

"—you're going off with her?" She couldn't help

it. Half a dozen friends had lived (or rather died) through this scenario.

"No, Sheila, no. I haven't seen her for ten years. I mean—" And then he blurted out, "She's dead."

To Sheila's shock and hurt was added consternation.

"For God's sake, Bob, why are you telling me all this? Am I supposed to write someone a letter of condolence? Have you lost your mind?"

I only wish, thought Bob.

"Sheila, I am telling you because she had a child."

"And we have *two*—so goddamn what?"

Bob hesitated. And then whispered, barely audibly, "He's mine. The boy is mine."

She stared in disbelief. "Oh, no, it can't be true." Her eyes were pleading for denial.

Bob nodded sadly: Yes, it's true.

And then he told her everything. The strike in France. The meeting with Nicole. Their brief affair. Then this afternoon. The call from Louis. And the boy. The problem with the boy.

"I really didn't know about it, Sheila. Please believe me."

"Why? Why should I believe anything you tell me now?"

He couldn't answer that.

In the awful silence that ensued, Bob suddenly remembered what he'd long ago confessed to her— so unimportant then. That he would like to be the father of a boy.

"*I wouldn't mind a little quarterback.*"

"*And what if it's another girl?*"

"*Well, then we'll keep trying. Isn't that the best part?*"

At the time they laughed. The "quarterback," of course, was Paula. And the operation at her birth made further children impossible. Sheila felt "unlovable" for many months. But Bob kept reassuring her, till gradually she once again believed that what they shared was far too strong for anything to change. They healed into an even tighter bond.

Until tonight, which was a requiem for trust. Now everything was a potential source of pain.

"Sheila, listen—"

"No. I've heard enough."

She rose and fled into the kitchen. Bob hesitated for a moment, then went after her. She was seated at the table, sobbing.

"Can I get you anything to drink?"

"No. Go to hell."

He reached out to stroke her blond hair. She moved away.

"Sheila, please . . ."

"Bob, why'd you have to tell me. *Why?*"

"Because I don't know what to do." *And because I somehow thought you'd help. And I'm a selfish bastard.*

He sat down across the table and looked at her.

"Sheila, please." He wanted her to talk. Say anything to end the ache of silence.

"You can't know how it hurts," she said. "Oh, God, I trusted you. I trusted—" She broke down again.

He longed to embrace her, make it better. But he was afraid.

"You can't forget so many happy years. . . ."

She looked at him and gave a tiny wistful smile.

"But that's just it," she said. "I've just discovered that they weren't happy."

"Sheila, no!"

"You *lied* to me!" she shouted.

"Please, honey. I'll do anything to make it right."

"You can't."

He was scared by the finality of her statement.

"You don't mean that you want to split. . . ."

She hesitated.

"Robert, I don't have the strength right now. For anything."

She rose from the table.

"I'm gonna take a pill, Bob. You could do me a big favor."

"Anything," he said with desperate eagerness.

"Sleep in your study, please," she said.

3

"WHO DIED LAST NIGHT, FOR HEAVEN'S SAKE?"

For once the gloomy philosopher Jessica had been wiser than she knew. They were in the kitchen eating—or in Jessie's case, dieting. She was ingesting Special K and half-and-half (half skim milk, half water), and commenting on the familial ambience.

"Eat your breakfast, Jessie," Sheila ordered, trying to feign normalcy.

"You look awful, Dad," said Paula with solicitude.

"I worked late," he answered, hoping that his junior wife would not detect that he had spent a sleepless night in his study.

"You work much too hard," said Paula.

"He wants to be world renowned," said Jessie to her sister.

"But he is already," Paula answered, then turning to Sheila for affirmation, "Right, Mom? Isn't Dad already famous everywhere?"

"Yes," said Sheila, "absolutely everywhere."

"Except in Stockholm," Jessie interposed, short-circuiting the flow of flattery.

"What's there?" asked Paula, taking Jessie's bait.

"The Nobel Prize, you idiot. Your father wants a

free trip to Sweden and a better table at the faculty club. Dig now, birdbrain?"

"Jessie," Sheila remonstrated, "don't insult your sister."

"Mother, her existence is an insult to any person of normal intelligence."

"Want this peanut butter in your face?" asked Paula.

"Stop it, both of you," said Bob. "The Nobel committee takes family manners into consideration."

"Oh, American men," sighed Jessica, somewhat out of the blue.

"I beg your pardon, Jessie," Sheila said.

"American men are absolutely driven by ambition. It's what makes them so provincial."

"Do you mind?" said Bob to Jessica.

"I was just being sociological, Father."

Paula stepped in front of Bob, to shield him from the verbal bullets of his hostile elder daughter.

"Dad, she likes to dump on you. But when you're not around she brags like anything. Just to impress the boys."

"I don't!" objected Jessica, her face now crimson with embarrassed indignation.

For a moment sibling rivalry allowed Bob and Sheila to forget their marital abrasions. They smiled at one another. Then they both remembered that this wasn't quite a normal morning. They withdrew their smiles—and hoped the children didn't notice.

"You drop his name to all the jockos on the football team," said Paula, pointing an accusatory finger at her sister.

"*Really*, Paula, you are fatuous," said Jessica, more than a bit discomfited.

"I'm not. I'm just as thin as you are, Jessie."

"Children, *please*," snapped Sheila, losing patience.

"There is only one child in this house," retorted Jessica, not noticing her mother's irritated mood.

"Ladies," interrupted Bob, "I'm driving both of you to catch the bus. Immediately." He gave a worried glance at Sheila.

"Okay," said Paula, scurrying to get her books.

"I'd like to go on record," Jessie Beckwith stated. "I'm against forced busing."

"But Jessie," said Bob, "this is to your own school."

Jessica looked at him. It was clear he hated her. Had no respect for her convictions. Indeed, she had lately come to suspect that he wasn't even her real father. Someday, hopefully, Sheila would confide to her that she and Sartre . . .

"Jessie, hurry up!"

But right now Sheila was still on *his* side.

He hovered by the door while the girls got ready.

"Uh—will you still be here when I get back?" he asked Sheila uneasily.

"I don't know," she answered.

She was still there.

"Are you leaving?"

"No."

"I mean, to work."

"No. I called the Press and said I'd work at home."

When he returned from ferrying the girls, she was still seated at the kitchen table, staring at her own reflection in a coffee cup.

I did this to her, he told himself, and was filled with self-loathing. He sat down across from her. She wouldn't start the conversation, so, after a long silence, he said:

"Sheila, how can I make it up to you?"

She slowly raised her head and looked at him.

"I don't think you can," she said.

"You mean we're gonna bust up over this?" he asked.

"I don't know," she said. "I don't know anything. I just . . ."

"What?"

"I just wish I had it in me to really hurt you back for this. I wish I could at least express my anger. . . ." Her voice trailed off. She had almost let slip that she was still, despite it all, in love with him. But that at least she would withhold.

"I know how you must feel," he said.

"Do you really, Bob?"

"Well, I have a notion. Christ, I wish I hadn't told you."

So do I, she thought.

"Why *did* you tell me, Bob?" She said it like an accusation.

"I don't know."

"You *do*, goddammit, Bob. You *do!*" Her fury was erupting. Because she knew now what he wanted from her. Damn him.

"It's the child," she said.

It struck him with a force that frightened him.

"I—I'm not sure," he said.

But she was absolutely certain.

"Look, Bob, I know you inside out. You didn't want it, you didn't plan it, but since you have it, you feel responsible."

He was afraid to ask himself if she was right.

"I don't know," he said.

"Bob, for heaven's sake, be honest with yourself. It's something that we simply have to face."

Clutching at straws, he interpreted her "we" as a

sign that she had not totally surrendered hope for them.

"Well?" She was waiting for an answer.

At last he mustered the courage to confront his feelings and admitted:

"Yeah. I do. I can't explain it, but I feel I should do something."

"You owe him nothing, actually. You know that, don't you?"

Yes, of course he knew ... objectively.

"He's all alone," said Bob, relieved that he could now confess his thoughts. "Maybe I could help to straighten out his life. Find some alternative to—you know, sending him away."

You're not his parent just because you screwed his mother, Sheila shouted to herself, but did not say anything.

"How exactly do you think you'd help?" she asked him.

"I don't know. But maybe if I flew there . . ."

"To do what? Do you know anyone who'd take him in? Do you even have a plan?"

"No, Sheila. No, I don't."

"Then what's the point of flying over?"

He could not defend his impulse. He could barely fathom it.

And then she staggered him.

"I guess there's only one solution, Robert. Bring him here."

He stared at her in disbelief.

"Do you know what you're saying?"

She nodded yes.

"Isn't that really why you told me?"

He wasn't sure, but he suspected she was right. Again.

"Could you bear it?"

She smiled sadly.

"I have to, Bob. It isn't generosity—it's self-defense. If I don't let you try to help him now, you'll someday blame me for allowing your—your child to be put in an orphanage."

"I wouldn't. . . ."

"Yes, you would. So do it, Bob, before I change my mind."

He looked at her. All he could manage as an answer was:

"Thank you, Sheila."

And so he let his lovely wife ignore the outrage and the imposition of it all as they discussed the visit of his son from France. The boy could join them when they moved down to the Cape.

"But just a month," she said. "Not one day more. That should give this Louis person ample time to make some permanent arrangement."

He looked at her.

"Do you realize what you're saying?"

"Yes."

He still could not believe it.

"What would we tell the girls?"

"We'll manufacture something."

God, how could she be so generous?

"You're incredible," he said.

She shook her head.

"No, Robert. I'm just thirty-nine years old."

4

Two weeks later, he was pacing back and forth in the corridor of the International Arrivals Building at Logan Airport.

In the strained and anxious days before, there had been many conversations with Louis Venargues. To make arrangements, establish the parameters for the boy's brief visit to America. A month, not one day more. And Louis would have to use this grace period to find some alternative to a state orphanage.

Louis had to tell Jean-Claude that he had been invited by old friends of his mother's. The idea was not totally implausible, since Nicole would surely have spoken to him about her year of residency in Boston.

But under no circumstances could Louis tell the boy that Robert Beckwith was his father.

"Of course, Bobbie. Anything you say. I know this is not easy for you. I understand."

Do you? Bob wondered.

Then there was the not inconsiderable matter of telling the girls. After much agonizing, Bob convoked a family meeting.

"A friend of ours has died," he said.

"Who?" asked Paula apprehensively. "Is it Grandma?"

"No," said Bob. "It's nobody you've met. Someone in France. A lady."

"A French lady?" Paula asked again.

"Yes," Bob replied.

Then Jessie said, "How come you're telling us if we don't know her?"

"She had a son , . ." Bob answered.

"How old?" Jessie quickly asked.

"Uh—roughly Paula's age."

"Oh wow," said Paula.

Jessica looked stilettos at her younger sister, and then turned to Bob. "And?" she inquired further.

"And he's an orphan," Sheila added with an emphasis that only Bob appreciated.

"Oh gee," said Paula sympathetically.

"That's why—" said Bob, "since he's alone—we'd like to ask him over for a while. Maybe a month. When we're in the big house at the Cape. That is, if neither of you minds."

"Oh wow," chirped Paula once again. Her vote was clearly yes.

"Jessie?"

"Well, there's justice in the world."

"What?"

"If I can't visit France, at least I'll have a native to discuss it with."

"He's only nine years old," said Bob, "and he'll be sort of sad. At least at first."

"But, Father, surely he can talk."

"Of course."

"Which means I'll hear a better French than Mademoiselle O'Shaughnessy's. Q.E.D. on you, Dad."

"He's my age, Jessie, not yours," Paula interrupted.

"My dear," said Jessie with hauteur, "he won't give you the *temps du jour*."

"The *what*?"

"Go study French. *Vous êtes une* twerp."

Paula pouted. Someday she'd get revenge on Jessie. And their foreign visitor would soon see what was what and pay attention to the true in heart.

Curiously, neither of them asked why the boy was crossing the Atlantic instead of staying with some friend who lived a little closer. But girls of nine are overjoyed to have a visit from a boy their age. And girls of twelve are anxious to gain worldliness through international experience.

Sheila made herself go through the motions of a normal day. Her act worked well enough for the girls, who seemed to sense nothing awry. She worked furiously, and actually completed the editing of Reinhardt's book. Bob, of course, could see behind this façade of industry, but could do nothing. Say nothing. As she grew more distant he felt increasingly helpless. They had never been estranged like this. At times when he was yearning for her smile, he would hate himself. At other times, he would hate the boy.

The Arrivals board announced that TWA 811 from Paris had just landed. A crowd began to form around the double-doored exit from the customs area.

And Bob suddenly was very scared. During the past weeks all the arrangements had occupied his mind to the exclusion of emotion. He'd been too distracted to allow himself to think what he might feel when those metal doors would open and a son of his would walk into his life. Not a theoretical dilemma he'd discussed by telephone, but flesh and blood. A living child.

The double doors now parted. Out came the flight crew, jabbering about the fantastic roast beef at Durgin-Park. And could they catch the Red Sox afterward?

"I know this disco . . ." said the captain, as they walked away.

In the instant when the open doors revealed the customs area, Bob craned his neck and tried to glimpse inside. He saw the lines of passengers, all waiting for inspection. But no little boy.

He was so distracted he began to smoke. Actually, since he had given up in high school, he was puffing on his pen. It pacified him somewhat, till he realized what he was doing. Embarrassed, he put it back into his pocket.

The doors now opened once again. This time a stewardess emerged, carrying a green leather valise and leading a tousle-haired little boy who was clutching a TWA flight bag close to his chest. The stewardess glanced swiftly at the crowd, finding Bob almost immediately.

"Professor Beckwith?"

"Yes."

"Hi. Guess I don't have to introduce you two." She turned to the boy, said, "Have a good time now," and slipped off.

Now, suddenly, the two of them were on their own. Bob glanced down at the little boy. Does he look anything like me? he thought.

"Jean-Claude?"

The boy nodded and held out his hand. Bob reached down and shook it.

"Bonjour monsieur," the child said politely.

Though his French was reasonably fluent, Bob had prepared some remarks in advance.

"Est-ce que tu as fait un bon voyage, Jean-Claude?"

"Yes, but I speak English. I have taken private lessons since I was small."

"Oh, good," said Bob.

"Of course, I hope to practice. I thank you for inviting me."

Bob sensed the boy's remarks had also been rehearsed. He picked up the green leather suitcase.

"Can I take your flight bag?"

"No, thank you," said the boy, clutching his red canvas sack even tighter.

"My car's just outside," said Bob. "Are you sure you have everything?"

"Yes, sir."

They began to walk. Through the doors and into the parking area, where the bright sun was now dimming into the afternoon. The humid Boston heat was still intense. The little boy followed silently, half a step behind.

"So the trip was okay, huh?" Bob asked once again.

"Yes. Quite long, but nice."

"Uh—how was the film?" Another question Bob had carefully prepared.

"I didn't watch it. I was reading a book."

"Oh," said Bob. They now had reached his car. "Look, Jean-Claude, a Peugeot. Doesn't that make you feel at home?"

The boy glanced up at him and gave a tiny smile. Did that mean yes or no?

"Would you like to sleep in back?" Bob asked.

"No, Mr. Beckwith. I would prefer to see the sights."

"Please don't be formal, Jean-Claude. Just call me Bob."

"I feel awake, Bob," Jean-Claude said.

Once they were inside the car, Bob asked him, "Do you know how to fasten your seat belt?"

"No."

"I'll help you."

Bob reached over and took hold of the belt. As he fumbled with it, drawing it across Jean-Claude's chest, he brushed him with the side of his hand.

My God, he thought. He's real. My son is real.

In a matter of minutes they were driving through the Sumner Tunnel and Jean-Claude was fast asleep. As they headed south on Route 93, Bob kept the car under the speed limit. The trip normally would take at least an hour and a half. But he wanted as much time as possible to look at the boy. Simply look.

The boy was curled up, leaning his head against the car door.

He looks a little frightened, Bob thought as he drove into the growing darkness. Hell, it's only natural. After all, he had woken up some twenty hours earlier in the sunny security of his native village. Was he afraid when he boarded the connecting flight to Paris that morning? Had he ever been outside the south of France? (That was a nice safe topic they might talk about tomorrow.)

Did someone from TWA meet him in Paris as promised? He had worried about that—a little boy changing planes all by himself. Did he know what to say? Well, obviously. And he seems to have such poise for a nine-year-old.

Nine. He had been alive for almost a decade without Bob's knowing he existed. But then *he* still doesn't know that *I* exist. Bob wondered what Nicole had told him of his father.

He looked at the sleeping child and thought, You are a stranger in a foreign land, five thousand miles from home and unaware that I, sitting right beside you, am your father. What would you say if you knew? Did you miss not knowing me? He looked at him again. Did I miss not knowing you?

The boy awakened just as they were passing Plymouth. He saw the road sign.

"Is that where the rock is?" he asked.

"Yes. We'll visit it sometime. We'll visit all the famous places while you're here."

Then the Cape Cod Canal. And Sandwich. The boy laughed.

"There is a place called *Sandwich?*"

"Yes." Bob chuckled with him. "There's even an *East* Sandwich."

"Who made up such a funny name?"

"Somebody hungry, I guess," said Bob. And the boy laughed again.

Good, thought Bob, the ice is broken.

Some minutes later, they passed another significant road sign.

"Now that is a reasonable name," said Jean-Claude, grinning mischievously.

"Orleans," said Bob. "Our Joan of Arcs all wear bikinis here."

"Can we go sometime?" he asked.

"Yes." Bob smiled.

WELLFLEET, 6 MILES.

Bob didn't want the trip to end, yet in a few short minutes, end it would. His wife and family were waiting.

"Do you know about my children, Jean-Claude?"

"Yes. Louis said you have two daughters. And your wife is very kind."

"She is," said Bob.

"Did she know my mother too?" he asked.

Jesus, don't ask Sheila that, Jean-Claude.

"Uh—yes. But distantly."

"Oh. Then you were her closer friend."

"Yes," Bob answered. And then quickly realized he should add, "I liked her very much."

"Yes," the boy said softly.

Just then they had reached the corner of Pilgrim Spring Road. In sixty seconds they'd be home.

5

THEY ALL STARED AT HIM WITH DIFFERING EMO-
tions.

Sheila felt an inward tremor. She thought she
had prepared herself for this. But she was not prepared. The little boy now standing in her living
room was his. Her husband's child. The impact far
exceeded everything she had imagined. Because, she
realized now, a part of her had been refusing to
accept the truth. But there was no escape now.
Proof was standing there before her, four feet tall.

"Hello, Jean-Claude. We're glad to have you."
That was the most that she could manage. Every
syllable took painful effort. Would he notice that
she couldn't smile?

"Thank you, madame," he answered. "I am very
grateful for your invitation."

"Hi, I'm Paula."

"Very glad," he answered with a smile. Her heart
was his.

At last the one aristocrat among them spoke.

"Jean-Claude, *je suis Jessica. Avez vous fait un
bon voyage?*"

"*Oui, mademoiselle. Votre français est éblouis-
sant.*"

"What?" Jessie had prepared herself to talk French, not to understand it.

And Bob watched as the youngsters spoke. He thought, My God, they're all my children.

"His English is terrific," said Paula to her sister, "and your French is terrible."

"Paula!" Jessie snarled, and sent her sister to the guillotine with filthy looks.

"*Terrible* is slang in French," said Jean-Claude diplomatically. "It also means terrific."

Jessica was reassured. This would be a splendid *continental* summer.

"Madame?"

Jean-Claude had now approached Sheila. Reaching into his flight bag, he withdrew a chunk of . . . clay? It looked like a heavy wad of ossified chewing gum. He offered it to her.

"Oh—thank you," Sheila said.

"What is it?" Paula asked.

Jean-Claude searched his vocabulary, but could not find the word. He turned to Bob.

"How do you say *cendrier?*"

"Ashtray," Bob replied, and suddenly recalled that Nicole smoked. In fact, it seemed that everyone in Sète had smoked.

"Thank you," Sheila repeated. "Is it—uh—handmade?"

"Yes," said the boy. "In our ceramics class."

"I take ceramics too," Paula said, to let him know how much they had in common.

"Oh," said Jean-Claude.

Golly, Paula thought, he's really handsome.

Sheila took the gift and looked at it. He'd meant well, after all. It was a touching gesture. A ceramic ashtray, signed by the craftsman who had made it: *Guérin 16.6.78.*

"*Voulez-vous boire quelque chose?*" asked Jessica,

ready to sprint for the cognac or mineral water or whatever beverage the Frenchman would fancy.

"Non, merci, Jessica. Je n'ai pas soif."

"Je comprends," she proudly said. This time she'd actually understood. Mademoiselle O'Shaughnessy, you'd flip your wig.

"How're things in France, Jean-Claude?" asked Paula, anxious to preserve her share of the guest's attention.

Bob thought it prudent to abridge this conversation.

"We'll have lots of time to discuss things, girls. But I think Jean-Claude's pretty tired. Aren't you, Jean-Claude?"

"A bit," the boy conceded.

"Your room's right across from mine," said Paula.

Jessie fumed. If Paula continued this inept vamping, she'd absolutely die of mortification. What would he think, for heaven's sake?

"I'll take his baggage up," said Bob to Sheila.

"No, I will," she replied, picked up the green valise (did it belong to *her*?) and said, "This way, Jean-Claude." She started up the stairs.

"Good night," he said shyly, and turned to follow her.

As soon as they were out of sight, Bob went to the liquor cabinet.

"Wow, he's cute!" gushed Paula.

"You are an acute embarrassment, Mademoiselle Beckwith," snarled Jessie. "You haven't got the foggiest notion how to address Europeans."

"Drop dead," said Paula.

"Come on, girls," said Bob, who had now fortified himself with Johnnie Walker. "Let's act our age."

For Jessie, *act your age* was the unkindest cut of all.

"Father, if you hate me, have the guts to *say* it like a man."

"Jessie, I love you." He put his arm around her, pulled her close and kissed her on the forehead.

"Your French is great, Jess. I had no idea you were so good."

"Do you really think so, Daddy?" Unbelievable. She sounded like a twelve-year-old, hungry for paternal approbation.

"Yes," said Bob, "I really do." And kept on hugging her.

"His English is fantastic," Paula said, "and he's only my age."

"He's had a private tutor," Bob explained.

"How come?" asked Jessie hopefully. "Is he noble?"

"No," said Bob. "His mother was a country doctor."

"What about his father?"

"I'm not sure," said Bob evasively, "but I know he wasn't noble."

"He's very independent," Sheila said.

"In what way?"

They were now in their bedroom. The rest of the household was already fast asleep.

"He wouldn't let me help him unpack. He insisted on doing it by himself," she said, and then added, "Was I cold to him?"

"No. How did you feel?"

"How do you think?"

"You were wonderful," said Bob, and reached out for her hand. She moved away.

"He took that little airline bag to bed with him.

Must have all his earthly treasures in it." There was distance in her voice.

"Guess so," said Bob, and wondered what a little boy of nine might carry with him as his consolation.

His eyes followed her as she went into the bathroom to brush her teeth. She emerged a few minutes later in her nightgown and bathrobe. Bob had lately gotten the disconcerting feeling that she was uneasy about undressing in front of him.

She sat down on the bed and started to adjust the alarm clock. (What for—wasn't this vacation?) He wanted to reach over and embrace her, but the gap of sheets and pillows separating them seemed much too wide to bridge.

"Sheila, I love you."

Her back to him, she kept playing with the clock.

"Sheila?"

Now she turned.

"He's got your mouth," she said.

"Does he?"

"I'm surprised you didn't notice."

Sheila slipped her robe off and burrowed under the covers. She lay silent for a moment, and then turned and said:

"She must have had brown eyes."

"I really don't remember."

Sheila looked at him, and with a melancholy smile said, "Come on, Bob."

Then she took her pillow and curled herself around it in the corner of the bed.

"Good night," she said.

He leaned across and kissed her on the cheek. She did not stir. He put his arm around her. She did not respond. He had vaguely hoped if they made love it would somehow make things better. He now saw that they were much too far apart for that.

He turned over on his side and picked up the

American Journal of Statistics. Better than a sleeping pill. He idly leafed through a particularly unoriginal piece on stochastic processes, and thought, Christ, I've said this stuff a million times. And then he realized that he himself was the author. It's still boring, he thought. I should've asked Sheila to tighten it up.

"Bob?" Her voice startled him.

"Yes, honey?"

He turned toward her. There was such pain on her face. And yet somehow she looked younger and so vulnerable.

"What exactly did I do—or rather not do?"

"Huh?"

"I mean, you never really told me why you did it."

"What?" He knew damn well, but wanted to buy time.

"What exactly was wrong with me that you had to have an affair?"

Damn, thought Bob. Why doesn't she understand that it was—what? Weakness? Chance? What could he say to mollify her?

"Sheila, nothing was wrong with you. . . ."

"With us, then. I thought we were happy."

"We were. We are." He said the last words with as much hope as conviction.

"We were," she said, and turned away again. To sleep.

Oh, God, thought Bob, this isn't fair. I can't even remember why it happened.

6

"Hey, Beckwith, there's some fantastic stuff at the mixer."

"I'm studying, Bernie."

"On a Saturday night with two hundred Vassar lovelies gracing our campus?"

"I've got midterms next week."

"So does everybody. That's why you need a piece of ass to loosen up."

Robert Alan Beckwith, Yale '59, put his math book down on the table and sat up on the moth-eaten couch of the Branford College suite he shared with Bernie Ackerman.

"Bernie, you talk like you get laid every weekend."

"I'm trying, Beckwith. At least you'll grant me that."

"Sure. You get an *E* for Effort—and a V for Virgin. Ackerman, you're pathetic."

"At least I take my swings, Bob. I try to score."

"But, Bern, you're batting zero. And I am too. But at least I don't make an asshole of myself. Besides, I came to Yale to get an education."

Bernie eyed his roommate.

"Listen, schmuck, this mixer's free of charge.

Doesn't that imply that Yale considers getting laid to be a part of the educational experience?"

"Bernie, I know myself. I'm shy. I lack your amazing charm and wit. I'm not competitive. . . ."

"In other words, you're scared."

"No, Bern. In those very words. I am scared."

And he buried himself once again in numerical analysis. Bernie simply stood there.

"Beckwith . . ."

"Bernie, go back to the mixer. Go get yourself blue balls. Just let me grind in ignoble peace."

"Beckwith, I'm gonna help you."

"Come on. You can't even help yourself."

"I have a secret weapon, Bob."

"Then you use it."

"I can't. I'm too short."

Bob looked up. Bernie had snared his interest.

"Willya come if I lend you my secret weapon? Willya, willya, willya?"

Bob once again sat up.

"What is it, Bern?"

"Willya come? Willya?"

"Okay, okay. The evening's shot anyway. I might as well get a free beer."

Bernie did not argue. The important thing was that he had persuaded Bob to drop his customary reticence and make the social scene. Who knows— with the secret weapon he might even score.

"I'll take a shower," Bob said, growing steadily more nervous.

"You took one after dinner, schmuck. Come on— we've only got an hour before the stuff is trucked back to Poughkeepsie."

"Can I at least shave?"

"Beckwith, you got about as much hair as a canned peach. Just put on the weapon and we'll enter the fray."

Bob sighed. "All right. Where is it?"

Bernie's eyes flashed with excitement.

"It's hanging in my closet. But shake ass."

Now he was hopping up and down.

Bob got his college blazer, combed his hair and washed his face. Then, after spilling Old Spice in every conceivable place, he reentered the living room, where Bernie stood like a midget colossus on the coffee table, holding . . . an article of apparel.

"That's it?" Bob frowned.

"Do you know what this is, Beckwith? Do you know, do you know?"

"Yeah. A goddamn *tie*."

"—which signifies that the wearer has won a varsity Y in *football!*"

"But I haven't," Bob protested.

"I have," Bernie said.

"You're the *manager*, Bern."

"Does it say that anywhere on the tie? Does it, does it, does it?"

"Bernie, I am a hundred-and-forty-five-pound weakling."

"But you're six one, Beckwith. Put two or three sweaters on under your jacket and you could be a tight end. Believe me, the girls know a football tie when they see one. It turns them on. They almost drop their pants right there."

"Bernie, forget it."

"Come on, Beckwith. This is your big chance."

"You ain't nothin' but a hound dog . . ."

It was pitch black, and the deafening sounds of Rumple and the Stiltskins shook the wooden panels of the Branford College dining hall. Bodies rocked and rolled. From either side, crowds of the opposing sexes glanced across at one another while pretending not to.

"Bernie, I feel like a total asshole."

"It's just nerves, Bob. The guys get 'em before every game. Christ, you look like Hercules."

"I'm roasting in these sweaters."

"Oh, Beckwith, lookit all the talent," said Bernie, surveying the populous scene. "God, I'm dying from the pulchritude. If we don't score tonight, we're goddam eunuchs."

"Speak for yourself, Bern."

"Hey! I see my beloved."

"Where?"

"There. The short and cute one. I've gotta make my move."

And for the final time he fixed Bob's tie and sprinted off.

Bob was now on his own. Too self-conscious to just stand there on the dance floor, he took one or two steps toward the female side. His eye now chanced upon a tall and slender girl with long blond hair. Boy, thought Bob, I wish I had the guts.

But three Yalies were already paying court to her. No chance, thought Bob. Besides, I'm really boiling. Maybe I should head back to the room.

"Beckwith!" someone bellowed.

It was one of the trio romancing the young lady. "Yes?"

"What the hell is that around your scrawny neck?"

To his horror, Bob now realized that the voice belonged to mountainous Terry Dexter, captain of the undefeated football team.

"Where'd you get that tie?" he bellowed, then turning to the Vassar girl, "He shouldn't be wearing that tie."

"Why not?" she asked, then turned to Bob. "What is it?"

"The Morons' Club." He smiled. God, she's beautiful.

"Like hell," said Terry. "It's the football team."

"Not much difference," Bob replied.

The Vassar girl laughed. This enraged the football captain.

"Beckwith, if you weren't such a fruit cake, I'd destroy you for that stupid witticism."

"Terry," interposed one of his sycophants, "the guy was only kidding. Don't make an asshole of yourself 'cause he's an asshole."

"Yeah," snarled Terry, "but at least take off that tie, Beckwith."

Bob sensed that this was one demand Terry would not be talked out of. Sweating profusely, he pulled it off and handed it over.

"See you, Terry," he said. And then, making swift retreat, Bob casually tossed a "Nice meeting you" in the direction of the lovely Vassar girl who had witnessed this horror show.

The moment he escaped into the coatroom area, Bob tore off his jacket. Thank you, Bernie, for this mortification. Dexter would doubtless never forget it. And you won't get your goddam tie back, either. As Bob was pulling the first of his sweaters over his head, he heard a muffled:

"Excuse me."

He peered out. It was the girl.

"Yes?" said Bob, too surprised to be nervous. He whipped the sweater back down.

"You forgot something," she said. And in her left hand she held out the football tie.

"Thank you. I guess I looked pretty stupid wearing it."

"No," she said gently. "I think it was the sweaters that made you look a little weird."

"Oh," he said. And then, "I'm just getting over a cold."

"Oh," she answered, perhaps believing him. "Why'd you leave?"

"I don't function well in mobs."

"Me either," she said.

"You were doing okay."

"Really? I felt like a piece of meat in a butcher's window."

"Well, mixers are always like that."

"I know," she said.

"Then why'd you come?" A stupid question. Bob instantly regretted asking it.

"I was going stir crazy up in Poughkeepsie," she answered. "Besides, can you imagine how depressing it is trying to study on a Saturday night in an all-girls' school?"

Say something, Beckwith! She asked you a question.

"Uh—would you like to take a walk?" God, I hope she doesn't think I want to lure her to the room. "Uh—I mean in the courtyard."

"Good idea," she said. "It's incredibly stuffy in there."

As they descended the stone stairway and strolled out into the chilly autumn evening, they introduced themselves.

"I'm Bob Beckwith. And as you probably can tell, I'm a math major."

"Are you always so self-deprecating?"

"Only with girls. I didn't catch your name."

"Sheila—Sheila Goodhart. And I haven't picked a major yet. Is that okay?"

"It's terrific, Sheila. It shows intellectual independence." She smiled.

They walked slowly around the courtyard. The band was barely audible.

"This college is so beautiful," she said. "It's like another century."

"Which reminds me," Bob replied, ignoring his non sequitur, "are you busy next weekend?"

"Yes," she said.

He was crushed.

"Oh."

"I mean with midterms. I've got to cram. How about the week after?"

"How about if I came up to Vassar next week and we studied together? I really mean study, Sheila, 'cause I'm a grind and I've got midterms too."

"Okay, Bob. I'd like that."

"Great." His heart was pirouetting.

Half an hour later, he walked her to Chapel Street, where the buses were waiting. Bob was in turmoil. To kiss or not to kiss, that was the question. At length he concluded that it would be best to play it safe. Why risk grossing her out?

"Well," he said as she was about to board the bus, "I look forward to next weekend. Uh—but I'll call you around the middle of the week. Like—er—maybe Wednesday at eight-fifteen. Okay?"

"Okay," she said and then, "So long." She turned and darted up the steps.

He watched her walk toward the back of the bus. She found a seat on his side, sat down and looked out at him. She was gorgeous even through a dirty windowpane.

He stood transfixed as the bus moved away from the curb, then down the street and into the New Haven night.

"Beckwith, where the hell've you been?"

"Out, Bernie."

"I was looking everywhere for you. Did you duck the mixer?"

"No."

"Well?"

"Well what?"

"What happened, goddammit, what happened?"

Bob waited. Finally he smiled and said, "Let's just put it this way, Bernie: The tie worked."

7

WHEN HE KISSED HER THE NEXT WEEKEND, IT WAS
all over. He knew for certain she would be the love
of his life. Don't ask precisely how. He just was
absolutely sure.

In the few minutes preceding that fateful embrace, as they were walking from the Vassar canteen
to her dorm, he made a final frantic attempt to dry
his palms. Again and again he rubbed them against
his sweater—to no avail. He could not, therefore,
reach for her hand. Instead he very casually put his
right arm around her shoulder. This accomplish-
ment, mentally rehearsed all that previous week,
was followed by a startling and unexpected develop-
ment: she put her left arm around his waist.

What does this mean? thought Bob.

To any casual observer, it had been an ordinary
college date. They sat opposite one another in the
library reading all afternoon, went off campus for
pasta at Francesco's, and returned to the library,
where they both, true to their words, really studied.
Not just their books, but each other.

There were the inevitable biographical details.
Sheila was the youngest of three daughters of a
Fairfield County physician. Her mother ("the only

Democrat in town"), was second-string art critic for the Stamford *Gazette*. Not only had her parents never divorced, they didn't even want to. Which is probably why both her sisters had married so young.

Bob's father had taught math at Penn for nearly forty years, during which time he published two textbooks and assembled a vast collection of jokes. ("Oh, that's where you get your sense of humor.") Bob's mother had died when he was barely seven, and Dan Beckwith thought it best to send his son to boarding school. Fortunately, Lawrenceville was less than an hour from Philly, so they could spend all their weekends together. Weekdays were pretty dismal, though, until the first form, when Bernie Ackerman arrived upon the scene. Even then he was a total madman, walking sports encyclopedia and fanatically loyal friend.

"Thanks to Bern, I met my future wife," Bob said to Sheila at dinner.

"Oh?" Her face was quizzical.

"You," he said.

She laughed.

"I'm not joking," he insisted.

"We've just met," she answered, looking away.

"Sheila, by their third date, Romeo and Juliet were already dead."

"You're crazy."

"Yes. About you."

This was over coffee and dessert. No further mention of matrimony was made that evening. Bob felt he had said it all. And Sheila felt he'd just been teasing her.

But she really liked him. Which is why she put her arm around him.

At the doorstep of Josselyn Hall there was the usual mob of couples, urgently getting in their final smooches.

"I wish you didn't have the long trip back to Yale," said Sheila.

"Ask me to stay," retorted Bob.

"You're never serious."

"That is where you're wrong, Miss Goodhart. I've never been more serious."

What happened next became the subject of debate for years to come. Who initiated that first kiss?

"I did," Sheila steadfastly maintained.

"Come on, Sheila, you were petrified."

"And you . . . ?"

"*I* was cool. But when I realized that you wouldn't sleep a wink that night, I put you out of your misery."

"Robert, don't make such a hero of yourself. I remember you just standing there, humming and hawing and blathering about exams, checking your watch every second—"

"Lies, Sheila."

"—and my heart melted."

"Ah."

"And I said to myself, If I don't kiss him now he may go catatonic."

"You make it sound like first aid."

"Well, I'm a doctor's daughter and I knew a basket case when I saw one. Besides, I was already in love with you."

"Then why the hell didn't you say so?"

"Because I was afraid you'd ask me to marry you again."

"So what?"

"I might have accepted."

"All right, Sheila, tell me everything."

"About what?"

"About the boy you were kissing."

"His name is Bob."

"Bob who, what, how and since when?"

The interrogator was Margo Fulton, self-styled mistress of letters, femme fatale, wit, purveyor of news and dispenser of worldly advice. The Aspasia of Josselyn Hall. Also the owner of a private telephone, which she allowed certain campus divinities to make use of. Sheila had been among those so honored in the days when she was going with Ken, her high school beau. (He had subsequently received a Fulbright to England and in Margo's words, "dumped you like the rat-head I always knew he was.")

"Well, Sheil, I'm panting for the details. Tell me all. Did he try anything?"

"I don't know what you mean, Margo," Sheila insisted.

"Oh, come on, don't be coy with your dearest friend." Margo's designation was, as usual, self-styled. "By the way," she added, "I had a fantastic weekend."

"Oh?" said Sheila.

Margo reluctantly gave in to this demand for full disclosure.

"I think it's love," she added. "I mean, it's passion for sure. His name is Peter, he plays polo, and he thinks I'm an absolute sex-bomb."

"Margo—you haven't . . ."

"No comment, Sheil."

It was rumored around the dorm that Margo was not a virgin. It was also rumored that she herself had started the rumor.

"How did you meet him?" Margo asked, suddenly changing the topic again.

"Last weekend at Yale. At a mixer, if you can believe it."

"A mixer! Good Lord, I haven't been to one of

those in years. Though actually I did meet Rex at one freshman year. You remember Rex?"

"I think so."

"He was an absolute volcano. I mean, Sheila, you have no idea. By the way, how tall is he?"

"Who, Rex?"

"No, your Yalie. I couldn't see how tall he was. He was bending over to, you know, kiss you."

Unwilling to provide Margo's rumor mill with the grist of Bob's vital statistics, Sheila answered with a question. "He's cute, isn't he?"

But Margo kept interrogating. "Is he sincere or just another rat-head sex maniac?"

"He's nice," Sheila answered. And thought to herself, He's really *really* nice.

"He looks like a basketball player. Is he?"

"I didn't ask him, Margo."

"Well, what on earth did you talk about?"

"Things," Sheila said, not wanting to betray a syllable of what they said to one another.

"Oh," said Margo, "that sounds *très piquant*. Anyway, you're a lucky woman if he's a basketball player. They make the best lovers. Or so they tell me. Actually, Douglas was a bit of a disappointment."

Sheila did not bother to ask who Douglas was, for she well knew that she was about to hear.

"Just because he was Princeton's high scorer, he thought he could score with me on the first date. A filthy-minded tiger-rat. Do you remember Douglas?"

"Yes, the Princeton star," Sheila offered.

"Well, he thought he was a star anyway. He had more arms than an octopus. I was so insulted I told him never to call me again. And do you remember what he did after that?"

"What?"

"He never called. Not even to apologize. Fink tiger-rat. Anyway, your Yalie's quite attractive. Do you think you'll . . ."

None of your dirty-minded business, Sheila thought. But since she'd always felt that Margo meant well underneath it all, she answered simply, "Time will tell."

"When are you seeing him again?"

"Next weekend. I'll be going there."

"Oh," said Margo. "By the way, does he have a friend?"

"I could ask. But I thought you were through with undergraduates."

"Yes, but I'm doing this for you, Sheila. You need the benefit of my experience."

"What you're saying, Margo, is that you haven't got a date next weekend. Right?"

"Well, as it happens, yes. Peter was too juvenile to ask me straight out. You can use my phone tomorrow if you like."

"Thanks, Margo," Sheila said, and yawned to give her friend a hint.

"Sweet dreams," said Margo. "We'll chat tomorrow."

At long last she left, to visit someone else for yet another soul-to-soul encounter.

Sheila lay back in her bed and smiled. I wonder if he's serious, she thought.

"Thanks for the car, Bern."

"Did you use it?"

"Obviously. I drove to Vassar—"

"I know you drove, schmuck. I mean the back seat."

Bob had to satisfy his roommate's intellectual curiosity.

"Yeah. I banged her twelve times."

"You're lying."

"Would you believe six?"

"Stop lying, Beckwith."

"Okay, Bern. The honest truth is that I kissed her. Once."

"Now I know you're lying."

It was after three and this was midterm week, but nonetheless Bob sat and fed his friend a few well-chosen vague details.

"I'm getting the impression that you like her, Beckwith."

"Well, I think I do." (To say the least!)

"Is she that great-looking?"

Of course she is, you asshole. You'd faint if she just looked at you with those green eyes. But I'm not giving you specifics. So Bob hid behind a little erudition.

"Remember Spenser's 'Epithalamion'? Well, she has that 'inward beauty which no eyes can see.'"

"In other words she's fugly, right?"

Bob smiled.

"Don't you think I could pick a winner, Bern?"

"Frankly, no. I mean, what would she see in you?"

"I don't know," Bob answered, poker-faced. He rose and started toward his bedroom.

"Where ya goin'?"

"To sack out. Good night." He closed the door.

Inside his tiny cubicle, Bob took out a leaf of Branford College stationery and wrote:

16 November 1958 (3:45 A.M.)

Sheila—

 I meant every word I said.

  Bob

8

THE FUNNY THING IS THAT THEY DID GET MARRIED. Not as soon as either of them wanted, but in June of 1960, one week after Sheila's graduation. Everyone was happy, though at times during their long engagement Sheila's mother, who "thought the world" of Bob, tried to convince her daughter not to hurry into matrimony.

"You're both so young. Why not live a little first?"

"I want to, Mother. But I want to live with *him*."

Dan Beckwith had no such hesitations. "She's a super girl," he told his son, "just super."

They honeymooned in the Bahamas, where Bob, unaccustomed to the tropics, got a serious case of sunstroke. His bride became his nurse.

"Maybe this is God's way of punishing us for not waiting till the wedding," Sheila said, almost half believing it.

Bob merely groaned and said, "Gimme some more Noxzema, huh?"

As she gently rubbed his blazing back, she once again posed the question of divine retribution for their premarital pleasures.

"Sheila," said the boiling lobster Bob, "even if the sunburn is a punishment, it's worth it for a year of making love to you."

She smiled and kissed his shoulder.

"Ow!" he said.

On their second anniversary, Bob asked his twenty-three-year-old wife if she had any regrets.

"Yes," she answered. "I should have married you the day you first proposed."

"You're together all the time," said Bernie once when he was up from Yale Law to visit. "Don't you ever—you know—get bored?"

"No," said Bob. "What makes you ask?"

"I mean, I sometimes get bored after two or three dates."

"Then you just haven't met the right girl yet."

"Shit, Beckwith, you're a really lucky bastard."

"Yeah, I know it."

Bernie was inspired. Three months after that, he got engaged to Nancy Gordon, an abridged edition of the former Sheila Goodhart. Everybody crossed his fingers. But it worked. In fact, they had a son within the year.

Neither Bob nor Sheila could recall a time when they had been without each other. They had walked hand in hand through what remained of college. And then in Cambridge, while Bob worked on his doctorate at MIT and she was hired by the Harvard Press, they walked hand in hand along the Charles. Once or twice a month they'd have a bunch of friends for dinner. They all, like Bernie, looked at Bob and Sheila and would yearn for a relationship like theirs.

And unlike their former classmates who were

going on in lit or gov or even medicine, they never had to scrounge. The U.S. Government was paying Bob's tuition and the U.S. Army paid him every summer just for the fun of solving statistical puzzles. And with what Sheila earned they could even afford such luxuries as season tickets to the Symphony. They could have traveled, for all Bob had to take along was his head, but Sheila wanted to spend the summers in Cambridge. Because she liked the place—and loved her job. She quickly rose from typing letters to proofreading galleys and then to editing actual books. On their fourth anniversary, she took Bob to dinner at Chez Dreyfus, insisting that it go on her newly acquired expense account.

"All you have to do is promise us your next book," she said, radiating professional satisfaction.

Next book? He hadn't written any yet. In fact, he hadn't even completed his thesis. But he felt so indebted to the Press for that $27.50 banquet that he flogged himself to finish it that summer. He made a book of it while teaching in the fall and had it accepted by H.U.P. before Sheila had to worry about their next anniversary dinner.

Not to be outdone, Margo made the (self-styled) marriage of the year to Robbie Andrews of the Ridgefield Andrewses. The lavishness of the wedding and the honeymoon was exceeded only by the lavishness of the divorce, sixteen months later. En route from the trauma to the Continent, she stopped off to see the Beckwiths at their "*très mignon*" Ellery Street apartment.

"My *God*," she whispered when Bob left the room with all the coffee cups. "He's got so—I don't know—mature. Is he lifting weights?"

"No."

"He must be doing something, Sheila."

Sheila gave a little smile and shrugged. But Margo caught the scent.

"Sheil, you're *blushing*."

"Am I?"

"Come on, Sheila, this is good old Margo. You can tell me. Is he an animal? Is he absolutely insatiable?"

"Let's change the subject, huh?"

"Oh, for God's sake, Sheila. Tell me or I'll die right on your brand-new rug!"

"Well . . . I guess we sort of *both* are."

And Margo blushed.

"To respond to another person when you are in pain, there must be a lot of trust between you."

Bob scribbled furiously.

"You don't have to write it *all* down," Sheila whispered.

"Shh—listen," Bob replied, and kept on scribbling.

The instructor, a slender athletic woman with a Dutch accent, had now completed her introductory remarks.

"Now, ladies, take your pillows and get on the floor. Gentlemen, you sit above them."

A dozen pregnant women dutifully sat in a circle on the floor of the Cambridge Adult Education Center as Ritje Hermans told them how to breathe their way through childbirth.

Bob was already feeling uneasy about this avantgarde approach to parenthood. What if I faint, he thought. He gazed at his lovely wife now rhythmically expanding and contracting at his feet and heard the subsequent instruction with intensifying anxiety.

"And don't forget your husband is the coach. He regulates and controls your breathing."

"Did you write that down, Bob?" Sheila smiled from the floor.

"Yes, honey."

"Don't forget, because I won't do anything unless you tell me to," she teased.

Great, he thought. Now I'm really gonna pass out.

As he was practicing the sacrolumbar massage on Sheila's back, Bob glanced around the room. Only in Cambridge could there be such an odd assemblage: a cabby, several students, a nervous neurosurgeon and an East African prince. Even an old geezer (must be over forty) with a youngish wife. The women shared a pride in their impending motherhood and the feeling that they looked like dancers in an elephants' ballet. The men shared the brotherhood of fear.

Except for the old guy. He was so involved. He even got down on the floor and did every exercise with his wife. Bob was almost jealous at his lack of inhibition. There was no way *he'd* let his wife down.

"Come on, Bob, you should have seen things from my angle."

This was after that first session. They were grabbing a quick burger at Mr. Bartley's.

"Well, what was the view from the floor?"

"I could see how they looked down at their wives. You know that cocky guy in the brown tweed jacket you think is so confident?"

"Yeah?"

"He doesn't even think the child is his."

"You're crazy."

"Trust me. He looked at his watch more than he looked at his wife. And he would've smoked if Ritje hadn't stopped him."

"How did I do?" Bob asked, really wanting reinforcement.

"How can I judge you, Robert? You're the loveliest husband in the whole world."

He kissed her and got relish on his lips.

They had barely moved into the new house in Lexington. They had their furniture, but less than half the books were up. New Year's Day 1966 was gusty with Arctic cold. Bob was staring out the window. I would hate to go out in this stuff, he thought.

Naturally, five hours later they were speeding down Route 2 toward Boston.

"Breathe easy, honey, and drive very carefully," he said.

"I am breathing, Bob. *You're* driving. So calm down."

He drove, but he could not calm down. By the time they reached the Lying In, his stomach cramps were synchronized with her labor pains. She squeezed his hand as he helped her from the car. "It's gonna be okay," she said.

In the labor room he timed her contractions and wrote them down. Through every one of them he tightly held her hand. Sometimes he stared up at the clock because he couldn't bear the sight of her in pain. She was so brave.

"Bob, you're a great coach," Sheila whispered.

As they wheeled her down the corridor he kept her hand in his.

"This is the home stretch, honey. Now I know we're gonna make it." Which was meant to tell her that he didn't think he'd faint.

She bore down when Dr. Selzer told her to, and soon a tiny head appeared.

Blinking from the glaring lights, Bob looked at it, half in the world, half still cocooned in Sheila.

Oh, my God, he thought, it's really happening. Our baby's real.

"Congratulations," Dr. Selzer said. "You've got a perfect little girl."

Since they had long ago decided on the names, she whispered to her husband through her tears.

"Oh, Bob, it's Jessica."

"She looks like you," he said. "She's beautiful."

He kissed the mother of his child.

9

HE MADE HIS BED HIMSELF."

An enchanted Paula was reporting to her mother the next morning.

"That's nice," Sheila answered, somewhat less impressed, "but what exactly do you find so amazing?"

"I was gonna do it for him."

"Really? Well, now *that's* unusual. You hardly ever make your own."

"I do too."

"Under duress."

"What's 'duress'?"

"Under pressure," Sheila Beckwith said by way of definition.

There were five of them at breakfast. Sheila fought to suppress the anger that she felt.

"Did you sleep well, Jean-Claude?" she asked.

"Yes, thank you, Mrs. Beckwith."

He was looking wistfully into his chocolate milk.

"Are you still hungry?" Sheila asked. "Is there something more you'd like?"

"No, thank you. That is . . ."

"Don't be shy," said Sheila.

"Well, at home we would drink coffee in the morning."

"Really?" Paula gasped, in awe of this sophistication.

"Of course," said Sheila. "I should have asked." She got up to get him some. He looked relieved and offered her his glass of chocolate milk in exchange.

"Today we're going to a barbecue," said Jessie. "Do you know what that is, Jean-Claude?"

"I think so."

"It's like a cookout," Paula added.

"Oh," said Jean-Claude. He seemed intimidated at the prospect. More strange new faces, he was doubtless thinking.

Paula continued enthusiastically. "There'll be hot dogs and hamburgers and corn on the cob with melted butter."

"Paula, you sound like a commercial for McDonald's," Jessie said sarcastically.

"Do you know what McDonald's is?" Paula solicitously asked Jean-Claude.

"Yes. It is a restaurant in Paris. I have eaten there."

The Peugeot was crowded as they all embarked for Truro, and the seaside home of Bernie Ackerman.

"He's been my pal since we were just about your age," said Bob to Jean-Claude, at whom he intermittently glanced through the rear-view mirror.

"He's a crashing bore," said Jessie. "All he ever talks about is sports."

"Jessica, behave yourself," said Bob sternly.

"He's a sportsman?" Jean-Claude asked, his interest piqued.

"Bernie is a lawyer," Bob explained. "He represents a lot of big-league athletes. Baseball, hockey, football—"

"Football?" Jean-Claude's eyes lit up.

"The American version," Jessie said disdainfully. "The breaking of empty heads."

Bob gave an exasperated sigh.

As they reached HOME PLATE, the sign for Bernie's place, it suddenly occurred to him that his wife had not said a word during the entire ride.

Sheila gazed at the kinetic patchwork quilt of T-shirts, jogging suits and summer dresses, and wondered if the friends she was obliged to greet with smiles would notice her unhappiness. Fortunately, everybody seemed preoccupied—sunning, tossing Frisbees, drinking, laughing, grilling, yelling at their children not to throw food. It was not a day for psychic scrutinizing. Probably she'd pull it off. At worst they'd think it was the lunar blues.

Bernie was the first to notice their arrival. He tapped Nancy on the shoulder and hurried toward them.

"Beckwith! Did you bring your catcher's mitt?"

"I left it in your garage last summer. How are you, Bern?"

The two old friends embraced.

"Sheila, you lucky thing, you look terrific." Nancy smiled. "Is it overwork or the Scarsdale?"

Thank God Nancy never really noticed. She once told Sheila she was looking marvelous while they were talking on the telephone.

As the salutations subsided, the Ackermans noticed an extra member of the Beckwith party. Bob hastened to explain.

"This is Jean-Claude Guérin, a visitor from France."

"Hi. I'm your Uncle Bernie, this is Aunt Nancy —and the tall kid over there sinking hook shots is my son, Davey."

"Very pleased to meet you," Jean-Claude said to them both. He held out his hand to Bernie.

"He's very cute," whispered Nancy Ackerman to Sheila.

"Does he play ball?" Bernie asked Bob confidentially.

"He's kind of tired from the plane trip, Bern. Besides, I don't think softball's big in France."

"Oh," said Bernie, and then loudly and slowly told the visitor: "You see, every year the fathers and the sons play softball. It's an annual event. Held every year."

"Oh," the boy replied politely.

"You're gonna love it," said the host, and added, "Beckwith, take your squad over to the feeding station. Give Jean-Claude a charbroiled burger. After all, this may be our last year. The surgeon general says the damned stuff's carcinogenic. Ice cream may be next. I'll see you guys in about an hour."

"Where you going?"

"Inside, back to the tube. The Sox and Yankees are tied two-all."

Bernie chugged into the house. Bob now turned to his "squad" to lead them to the barbecue pit. But Jessica had already wafted off. And Sheila was —or seemed—deep in conversation with Nancy Ackerman and the psychiatrist next door.

Paula and Jean-Claude had waited loyally.

"Come on, Dad," said Paula, tugging at his arm. "Let's start having fun."

"Wanna go to a movie sometime, Jess?" asked Davey Ackerman.

"The name is Jessica. And no, I wouldn't. I don't go out with juveniles."

"I'm fourteen months older than you."

"Chronology's irrelevant."

"You think you're a hot shit but you're not, Jessie. Besides, there are lotsa fish in the sea."

"Good. Go marry a fish."

"I'm not marrying anybody. I'm gonna be a professional ball player."

"I couldn't care less, David," Jessica retorted, and then, "What sport?"

"I'm deciding between baseball and basketball. Or maybe pro soccer. My dad says soccer's gonna be huge in the eighties. I can kick with both feet."

"Not at once, I assume," said Jessica.

"Very funny. You'll be sorry when I'm a superstar."

"Don't count on it, creep."

When it came to Jessica Beckwith, the normally pugnacious Davey Ackerman, who would slug at the drop of an epithet, had the patience of a saint. If only Jessie weren't so darn good-looking, he might cure himself of the painful crush he had on her. Or if only she'd recognize his many athletic virtues. But as things stood, he was violently jealous of everything that caught her attention, even inanimate objects like books. Small wonder, then, that he now fixed upon the presence of Jean-Claude Guérin.

"Who's that foreign kid?"

"He's from abroad. A visitor."

"Who's he visiting—you?"

"Well, let us just say the Beckwith family, of which I am a member."

"Where's his parents?"

"None of your business. Actually he's an orphan," said Jessica.

"No shit," said Davey. "You guys gonna adopt him?"

This had never occurred to Jessica.

"I'm sorry, but I'm not at liberty to say."

* * *

"Play ball!"

At last the annual Bernie Ackerman Cape Cod Invitational Softball Game was under way. Parents and children had been split into two teams, led by Bernie and Jack Ever, a computer scientist. Bernie won the toss and got first draft choice. Purely on ability and all-important killer instinct, he selected Davey Ackerman.

Bob was chosen by Jack Ever on the seventh round. Though a distinguished academic, he was, as Bernie had to tell him candidly, a pretty mediocre catcher. The signing up of Nancy Ackerman and Patsy Lord as short-center fielders made the contest nominally coed. Paula Beckwith joined the senior citizens and toddlers seated on the first-base line, prepared to cheer her daddy. Jessica sought solitude beneath a tree with Baudelaire (in English). Hardly in a sporting mood, Sheila went to walk along the beach.

The shore was empty. Far up the beach, a solitary child was playing in the sand. But that was all.

She had realized something in the moment that they reached the party. Seeing all their friends and pseudo friends, she knew at once that things would never be the same. Not just because they all looked up to her and Bob. To hell with images. But Bob was no longer funny, loving, faithful Bob. Ever since she'd seen that child, the one certainty that had defined her life had disappeared.

God, she thought, how smug I must have been. All around us marriages were splitting or relationships eroding and I'd taken ours for granted. We were different. Unchanged, unchanging and unchangeable. Was it *hubris* to feel so secure? Is that where I went wrong?

She walked in the direction of the solitary child.

And now, to her dismay, she saw it was Jean-Claude, sitting on his haunches, digging in the sand. She slowed. She didn't want to have to talk to him. But from this vantage point she could observe him without being seen.

You know, we have a lot in common, Sheila thought. We both were happy once.

And numbed by melancholy, she fantasized a conversation they might have if they were meeting for the first time here, alone on this deserted beach.

"Hello, whose little boy are you?"

"My mother is Nicole Guérin, my father's Robert Beckwith."

"Really? Robert Beckwith is my husband."

"Oh?"

"That sort of complicates things, doesn't it?"

Just then the little boy looked up, saw her, and waved. I know it isn't your fault, Sheila forced herself to think. She waved back. He looks so sad.

But then it isn't my fault either, dammit. She turned and walked along the shore away from him.

Tension was mounting. The score was 12–12 and they were into extra innings. Both teams were wilting from the heat, but no one more than Bob, who had been roasting in his catcher's mask. It was bottom of the tenth and Bernie's team was batting. Davey Ackerman had lined a double to left field and now was dancing boldly from the base. Once or twice Bob thought he might rifle the ball to the second baseman and catch Davey off guard, but his arm was sore just from returning the ball to the pitcher.

Now Bernie was in the batter's box.

"Come on, Dad, send me home!" called Davey, as he hopped up and down and whistled to encourage his father and distract the pitcher. Bob signaled for a low fast ball, which, alas, came in shoulder high and slow.

Bernie's swing caught just a piece of it and popped a fly to shallow center. The instant Patsy Lord caught it, Davey Ackerman was off and flying toward third base. And it was clear that he would try to score. Patsy fired the ball to Bob, who had thrown off his mask and stood astride the base line, blocking home plate. But Davey rounded third and fearlessly charged homeward.

"Knock his head off, Davey!"

This parental counsel came from Bernie, shrieking like a maniac.

Davey was a cannonball aimed straight at Bob. As he drew near, Bob lunged to tag him, but couldn't. Davey dodged, and slid right into him. Bob fell backward on the ground. The softball trickled from his glove. The other team was cheering. They had won!

"No hard feelings," Bernie crowed at Bob. "Are you okay?"

"Yeah," Bob said, slowly getting up. He gritted his teeth. *That little bastard.* He wiped the dirt and sweat off with his sleeve and walked away. *Shit, my shins are aching.*

"Are you all right, Daddy?" It was Paula, who had sprinted to her father's side.

"Don't worry, sweetie. I'll just get some water on my legs. See you in a sec."

As the players all stampeded for the beer and Cokes, Bob stopped, untied his sneakers and walked toward the beach. Just where grass ended and sand began, he saw the visitor from France perched on a dune. Jean-Claude looked concerned.

"Did he hurt you, Bob?" he asked.

"No, it's nothing."

"Is it permitted, what he did?"

"Yes. I was too slow. I should have tagged him and gotten out of the way." He patted the boy on the head.

"Do you want to get your feet wet in the ocean?"

"Yes."

They walked together to the water's edge. He waited for Jean-Claude to take his shoes off and they waded in. Bob grimaced when the water reached his shins.

"I would like to hit that boy," said Jean-Claude, looking away.

Bob laughed. And thought, Me too.

10

H<small>OW WAS YOUR DAY</small>?"

"Not bad," Sheila answered tonelessly. She was combing her hair as they both prepared for bed.

"Not good, either, huh?" said Bob, applying ice in towels to his aching shins. He looked at her. Even in her faded bathrobe and with night cream on her face, she was beautiful. He wanted her so badly.

"No, Robert, certainly not good." It was always in times of extreme emotion that she called him Robert. In the midst of making love, and when she was really angry.

"Do you think anyone suspected?" he asked.

"What?"

"Did they—uh—wonder who he was?"

"I don't think so. Anyway, I couldn't give a damn."

Yeah, she was very angry.

"Sheila, I—"

"What's important, Bob, is that *I* knew."

"I understand."

"You don't. You haven't any notion of how hard this is for me." She sat down on the bed and stared across at him. "I can't take it, Robert."

He was about to remind her that she had volunteered, but stopped himself. After all, he was the culprit.

"Then maybe we should send him home?" He looked at her hopelessly.

She examined the ends of her long hair. An activity to keep her mind off castigating him. To keep her deep resentment from erupting into words.

"Look, I said I would and I will," she replied, still looking down, "but . . ."

"But what?"

"I'm going to need a little relief. It's impossible to just pretend that this is some everyday occurrence. It's not, and I'm going to have to get away now and then."

"Of course." What could she mean? Her words unsettled him.

"Tomorrow. I want to go to Boston for the day."

"Oh, good. A good idea," said Bob, relieved that she had not demanded even more time.

She put her hairbrush down on the night table, turned out the light and climbed under the covers, her back to him. She was still wearing her bathrobe.

He reached over and put his hand on her right shoulder. Just a friendly touch, he told himself. In fact, it was an interrogatory gesture.

"I took a pill, Bob," she said very softly, without turning.

I only want to . . . he was going to say. But that was not the truth and she would know it. It would make things even worse.

In a minute she was sleeping. She had deserted him. He turned to his own night table and rummaged for a magazine. He found a year-old issue of *Boston,* and immersed himself in it.

But reading only made him more awake. Perhaps it was the survey of good coffeehouses in the city.

Vicarious caffeine. In any case, he felt too restless to remain in bed. He got out quietly, glancing over at his wife who was in deep if troubled sleep, put on his slippers and left the room.

It was cold in the house, and at the top of the stairway he took his jogging jacket from the hook, zipped it up and started down the stairs.

In the living room he saw the boy.

He was seated in pajamas on the sofa, staring out the window at the ocean.

"Jean-Claude?" Bob said softly.

The boy turned quickly, somewhat startled. "*Oui —yes?*"

"Are you all right?"

"Yes. I couldn't sleep."

"That makes two of us," Bob answered. "Aren't you cold?"

"A little."

Bob removed his jacket, wrapping it around the boy's shoulders.

"Thank you," said Jean-Claude.

"Would you like a glass of milk?"

"Yes, please."

"Come on."

He sat at the kitchen table as Bob poured some milk into a pan and started heating it. While it warmed, he opened up a beer. Then he gave Jean-Claude the milk, and sat down with him. It was very quiet in the house. They could hear the ocean.

"Did you enjoy today, Jean-Claude?"

The little boy looked lost and sad. "I am sorry that I don't know baseball."

"It's not important," Bob replied, and added, "As you could see, I don't know too much baseball, either."

Silence. Jean-Claude sipped his milk.

"What were you looking at when I came down? The sea?"

Jean-Claude hesitated, and then answered, "Yes, I was wondering how far it was . . ."

". . . to France?"

"Yes."

"Too far to swim." Bob smiled, and then, "Are you homesick?"

"Well, a little. When I look out at the water I imagine that I see my village."

Bob felt sorry for him.

"Come on. Let's go back and look out at France."

The boy padded after Bob back to the living room. He sat on the sofa once again, Bob in the easy chair right near him.

"It's a lovely village, Sète."

"Do you know it?" asked Jean-Claude.

Bob sensed this would be the first of many innocently probing questions. But he felt a need to talk, if only indirectly.

"I was there once," he replied, "many years ago."

The next question, though inevitable, still made Bob's heart beat faster.

"Did you know my mother there, or just in Boston?"

Bob hesitated. Something in the verb "to know" stirred deep emotions in him. Well, what should the story be—platonic friendship in the States or casual acquaintance on a trip to France?

"Uh—just in Boston. When she was a resident at Mass General. We met at someone's house."

The little boy's eyes brightened.

"Did you like her?"

How should he answer?

"She was very nice," Bob offered.

"She was a very good doctor," the little boy

added. "We could have lived in Paris, but she preferred the south."

"I know," said Bob. And wondered suddenly if these two syllables had not been too revealing. But the boy said nothing for a moment. Then finally:

"We would go camping sometimes, just *Maman* and I. We went to Switzerland at Easter and she promised next year I could have skiing lessons. . . ." His voice trailed off.

Bob wondered what to say.

"You can still take lessons."

"I don't want to now."

Life goes on, he stopped himself from saying. What an idiotic thing to tell a lonely child.

They sat in silence. Bob had drained his beer and wanted to get another. But he couldn't leave the boy alone.

"Did you know my father?"

Though he knew it had to come, it nonetheless sent shivers up his spine. What did the child know really? Had Nicole, had Louis . . . ?

"Did you, Bob?"

He was still unsure how to answer.

"Uh—what did your mother tell you about him?" He braced himself to hear the answer.

"That he was married to someone else." The boy lowered his head.

"And?" Bob's heart was hammering.

"That she loved him. And they loved each other and decided to have me. But of course he could not stay in France."

"Uh—did she ever tell you who he was?"

"No. But I have my own idea."

"What?"

"I think perhaps he was an Englishman."

"Why do you say that?"

"Because if he was Italian, I think she would

have made me learn Italian. So I could someday talk to him."

Bob's next thought embarrassed him. For in the early hours of morning, his guard was lowered and he told himself, How logical he is: sort of like me. The boy continued wistfully.

"I always hoped that maybe when I was grown up, *Maman* would . . ."

". . . tell you all about him?"

"Yes. But now she's dead."

For the first time since he arrived, he had explicitly referred to his mother's death. And his own words caused the child to burst into tears.

Silent, choking sobs that shook his little body.

Bob's heart was aching for the child. He longed to lift him up and take him in his arms.

At last he did.

The little boy responded instantly. He threw his arms around Bob's neck and clung to him.

"*Maman,*" he murmured, crying all the while.

"I know," Bob answered softly, rocking him. "I know."

They held each other tightly, neither wanting to let go. Until their intimate embrace was interrupted.

"Bob?"

It was Sheila, standing sleepily on the first step.

To Bob, his wife's expression seemed to reflect betrayal.

Slowly, he let the boy slide onto his feet.

"Sheila—are you okay?"

She was slightly woozy from the pill.

"I woke up and you were gone," she said.

"I couldn't sleep. Jean-Claude was sitting here when I came down."

"Oh," she answered hoarsely.

"We'll all go to bed now," Bob said quickly.

"That's all right," she answered blankly. "I was just a little worried."

And she turned and walked back up the stairs. Bob's eyes followed her as she disappeared. For a moment he had forgotten the child. His vacillating emotions were now fixed on what his wife might be thinking and feeling.

Then something touched his hand. He looked down.

"Bob," the little boy said, "I think I will go to bed now."

"Good. A good idea." Bob bent down and once again the child embraced him. He was too much in conflict to respond.

11

SHEILA DARLING, WHAT A LOVELY SURPRISE. I thought you'd be stuck on the Cape for the whole bloody month."

"Thanks. You're the best thing that's happened to my ego this week."

"Lovey, ego-boosting is my middle name."

Well, not exactly. Sheila's former college classmate was now Margo Fulton Andrews Bedford van Nostrand. She was nursing a martini in the patio of Harvest, the new restaurant behind the Brattle Theater, where she had a daily noontime table.

"Is this mine?" asked Sheila, indicating the glass of tomato juice sitting before her.

"Yes. Your usual."

"I think I'd like it spiked today," said Sheila.

"Good," said Margo, and signaled Perry. "Unvirgin this, please." He nodded and went off for a jigger of vodka.

"Well, how's Bob and the girls?"

"Fine. They all send their love," Sheila answered. In fact, she had told the children she had business at the Press. And had told Bob nothing. "How's Hal?"

"Hal is Hal, to paraphrase Gertrude Stein, and

he always will be. That's why I married him. No
risk of surprises."

"And how's the gallery?"

"Obscene." Margo grinned. "I mean, it gets more
successful every week. Hal is flabbergasted. He
really thought it would just be a whim with me and
I was too scatterbrained to be anything but a pretty
face. Now he says I have a better business head
than he does. Anyway, what brings you back to
Cambridge? Isn't this your holiday?"

"Yes, but I had some things to take care of. Uh—
shall we order before it gets impossibly crowded?"

"Darling, you know I always have their special.
Saves small talk with Perry—who, you've probably
noticed, has a teeny crush on me. I've ordered for
you as well."

"Fine," said Sheila, not bothering to inquire
what she would be eating. "Is that a new dress? It's
very chic."

"It is, but you've seen it half a dozen times.
What's with you today?"

"Nothing," said Sheila, taking a sip of her Bloody
Mary.

"Are the girls okay?" Margo asked.

"Of course."

"Bob?"

"Of course. You already asked me."

"Yes, but I wasn't satisfied with the answer. You
look preoccupied, Sheil."

In the long-ago college days, Margo had always
talked as if watching herself in a mirror. As she grew
older, she began redirecting her considerable analyt-
ical gifts to those around her. Narcissism, once her
all-embracing way of life, was now merely an occasional indulgence. Sheila was to a great extent responsible for this evolution. Her example had
inspired Margo to relate to other people.

"Come on, Sheila, 'fess up. Is something wrong?"

"Yes."

"What? Tell me."

As Sheila removed her sunglasses and covered her face with her hand, Margo could see she had been crying.

"What happened?" she asked apprehensively.

"Bob had an affair." Sheila said it quietly and quickly and then lowered her head.

"Oh, God, Sheila, I don't believe it. Bob is simply not the type. He thinks he's Adam and you're Eve. He wouldn't. Believe me, darling, I'd know the vibes. Bob wouldn't."

"He did," Sheila said almost inaudibly.

"Come on, I read about this syndrome in *Psychology Today*—or was it *Passages*? It's common at your age."

"*Our* age," Sheila interrupted with a little smile.

"Well," Margo temporized (she was "midthirties" and intended to remain so for some time to come), "women near their forties have this kind of lapse in confidence. They start to imagine—"

"It's not my imagination."

"Oh?"

Sheila raised her head.

"He told me."

"Oh."

Margo looked at her former roommate and, with genuine shock in her voice, added, "This is really upsetting, Sheil."

"I know," said Sheila, who had hoped Margo might be a little less emotional and more dispassionately comforting.

"Listen, they sometimes lie. When I told Frederic I was having an affair with Hal, he told me *he* was seeing someone in New Jersey—which was a total fabrication. A fictive tat for my very real tit. Can you imagine, New *Jersey?*" And then, upon further reflection, she added, "Of course, Bob is more mature than Frederic. He's straight as an arrow. Why would he tell you such a wounding thing if it weren't the truth? Sheil, he must be telling the truth."

"He is."

"But why? You've always been so happy." Margo looked at Sheila's weary face.

"The honeymoon is over, Margo." She could not help sounding bitter.

"Sheila, this is absolutely shattering," said Margo, implying that the news was also shattering *her* few remaining illusions. "Who the hell did he fall for?"

"She was French."

"Ah, I might have known," said Margo, too upset to notice Sheila's use of the past tense. "It would have to be a *français,* wouldn't it?"

"*Française,*" Sheila quietly emended. It was a reflex. She had regressed to the state of copy editor.

Margo sat silent for a moment, not knowing how to respond. At last she said, "I'm really sorry, Sheila."

Then Sheila gave voice to her greatest agony.

"They had a child."

"That's impossible. Are you sure?"

"Yes. Very."

"Oh, Christ," Margo said as quietly as she could manage, and then, "But *why?*"

"Bob claims he didn't know."

"Do you believe him?"

"Yes. I think I do."

"Well, what's the French creature's excuse?"

"I don't know," Sheila mumbled. "She's dead."

"What?" Now Margo was totally confused. "You'd better tell me everything. From the beginning."

As she recited the events in sequence, Sheila grew more and more angry. This is so monstrous. What am I doing in this nightmare? Margo took it all in, her eyes widening. When Sheila got to Nicole's death and Bob's confession, Margo could no longer suffer in silence.

"God, Sheila, this beats everything I've ever heard. I thought Bob was perfect."

"So did I," said Sheila sadly.

There was a pause. Neither woman knew quite what to say.

"Well," said Margo, desperately trying to find a bright side, "at least you don't have to worry about losing Bob. Did she call the child Beckwith?"

"No."

"Well, maybe you could pretend it's World War Two and Bob was a GI in Europe and—"

"And?"

"And let the matter drop. A lot of women did in those days."

"I can't. Bob wanted to see the boy."

Margo was offended. This was an unconscionable breach of propriety. "God, men are pathetic. They really get off on the idea of boy children. I hope you put your foot down, Sheila. Him or you."

"That's precisely what I didn't want, Margo. If I made him choose, there'd always be a chance I'd lose him."

Margo eyed Sheila with mounting anxiety.

"What the hell did you do?"

She told Margo the rest of the story.

"Sheila, you are stark, raving mad."

"On the contrary, I'm stark, raving *realistic*. I have the girls to think about."

"But in your own *home*, Sheil. Where can it lead?"

"Look, we made a bargain. One month and the

boy goes back to France. There are some people trying to make arrangements for him. Better thirty days of suffering than a lifetime of uncertainty."

"But how the hell can you stand it?"

Sheila shrugged.

"I don't know. Sometimes I can't. Sometimes when we're sitting there at night pretending to listen to Bach and pretending to read and pretending that everything is the way it always was, I feel such *rage* that I could kill him—"

"Maybe you should," Margo interrupted sardonically.

"—and yet there are other times when I feel I need him more than ever. Strange, isn't it? Even after what he's done, he's still the only one who can really comfort me."

Margo looked at her and shook her head. "I can't understand you, Sheil."

"Neither can I," she replied. "But love and hate don't seem to cancel each other out. They can coexist and drive you mad."

Margo shook her head again and sighed.

"And do you really believe that it'll be all wrapped up neatly at the end of the month?"

"Yes. That was our agreement," said Sheila. But in her heart she feared that Margo might be right. She was no longer sure of anything.

"What do the girls think?"

"We didn't tell them who he was. They think he's cute."

"Is he?"

"I don't know."

"Don't you look at him?"

"As little as possible, frankly. And when I do, my only reaction is 'What did she look like?' Am I crazy, Margo?"

"No, darling," she answered, reaching across the

table and touching Sheila's hand affectionately. "You're the wisest woman I know. If Hal ever did that to me, the only thing I could do is go out and have an affair or shop. Or both. I'd never have the strength to face it the way you have. It's a gamble, but knowing you, you'll shame Bob into line with your generosity. Now, can I help?"

"How?"

"However you want. God knows you've seen me through enough crises. I'll come down—"

"No, it's bad enough I have to go back."

"Do you? Can't you stay a few days with Hal and me?"

She shook her head. "Margo, you're a friend. But I've got to face it."

"God, I envy you," said Margo.

It was hardly the conclusion Sheila had expected. "Why, for heaven's sake?" she asked.

"I wish I could love a man as much as you love Bob."

"Thanks, Margo. Thanks for understanding."

12

THE SUN WAS SOFT AND WARM. GENTLE WAVES nuzzled the shore of Cape Cod Bay. The little boy was sitting by himself, one of Bob's baseball caps on his head, a book in his hands.

"Hi, Jean-Claude."

He looked up. It was Paula Beckwith. "Hello."

"Whatcha reading?" she asked, peering at his book.

"*Histoire Générale*—world history," he replied.

"Wow! You must be very intellectual."

"Not really." He smiled. "Would you like to sit down?"

Paula plopped onto the sand as she answered, "Sure." She quickly settled in for a friendly chat.

"What's new in history?" she asked.

"I am reading about Vercingetorix."

"What's that?"

"He was the first French hero. He led a revolt against Julius Caesar."

"I've heard about Julius Caesar, I think. What happened after that?"

"He ended badly. Caesar had him strangled."

"Ugh." Paula clutched her neck in empathy for

the valiant dead man. "Do they let you read that kind of stuff in France—gory, I mean?"

Jean-Claude shrugged.

"Are there pictures in that book?"

"Yes."

"Is there one of the strangling?"

"Uh—no. I'm sorry."

Paula pondered for a moment. "We take hygiene next year," she said.

"What is that?"

"Do you know what 'sexual education' is?"

"I think so." He wasn't quite certain and didn't want to admit it.

"Do you have that course in France?"

"I'm not sure."

"Well, do you know where babies come from?" she asked, enjoying the thrill of grown-up dialogue.

"Uh—yes."

"Who told you—your mom or your dad?"

"My mother. She was a doctor."

"Yeah, I know. How come your dad didn't tell you, though?"

Paula had innocently trespassed onto Jean-Claude's most private anxiety.

"My father was not there," he said, and hoped she'd change the subject.

"You mean he was dead already?"

"What?"

"My father said your father was dead."

"Oh," said Jean-Claude, wondering why Bob's version should have contradicted what his mother had always told him. "Well . . ." His voice trailed off.

Meanwhile, Paula was preparing to probe deeper.

"What's your favorite color?" she asked.

"The color of the sea," he answered.

"But it's not one color. Sometimes it's green and sometimes it's blue."

"Well," he replied, "that's what I like."

"Cool," said Paula. "You're a really fascinating person, Jean-Claude."

"Thank you. You are also."

"Really? Do you really think so? Hey—was that French you were speaking on the phone just now?"

"Yes," the boy replied, a trifle uneasy.

"It sounds terrific. I'm gonna start it in sixth grade. Then I'll be able to visit you sometime."

"That would be very nice."

"Yeah," said Paula, happy to receive the invitation. "Uh—were you talking to a friend?"

"Yes."

"Boy or girl?"

"Neither."

"Your dog?" She was serious. Jean-Claude laughed.

"No, an old friend of my mother's. Louis Venarguès. He was mayor of our village for many years."

"Wow," said Paula. "What does he talk to you about?"

"Oh, this and that. He says he will call every week to ask me how I am."

"Gee, I wish I had a friend like that."

The boy looked wistful and his eyes were saying, You have parents. But Paula didn't notice. In fact, just then she bounded up as swiftly as she had plopped down.

"Hey, I gotta help Jessie cook."

"Oh," said the boy, who now was not anxious to be left alone again. "What are you cooking?"

"Stuff," said Paula.

"What kind of stuff?" he inquired, showing serious interest.

"We're making dinner to surprise my mom when she gets home. You wanna watch?"

"Yes," Jean-Claude replied, and leaped to his feet.

As they started toward the house, side by side, their arms occasionally brushed. And Paula Beckwith inscribed the joy she felt upon a special page of memory. To prize forever.

Julia Child was spread out on the kitchen table.

Jessica was poring over it, surrounded by open jars, boxes, bottles, and piles of assorted vegetables. Bowls and spoons were scattered everywhere.

"Dammit, Paula, where've you been? I've been killing myself all afternoon!"

Her little sister entered, with Jean-Claude a step behind. Seeing him, Jessie restrained her anger.

"Hi, Jean-Claude—"

"Yuck," said Paula, interrupting. "What a mess in here! Whatcha doing, Jessie—cooking or finger painting?"

"Paula, I am trying to make a *blanquette de veau*. It's taken me *hours,* and all you've done is criticize."

"Well, what do you want me to do?"

"Nothing." Jessica sighed with exasperation.

Paula turned to Jean-Claude and explained, "Jessie's studied cooking in school."

"Oh," said the visitor.

"That was nothing," Jessie sniffed. "Our fanciest project was macaroni and cheese."

"Wish you'd made that," Paula murmured. "At least we'd be able to eat it. What's all that junk on the stove?" She pointed to the four pots, all steaming like a grade school production of *Macbeth.*

"Well, Jean-Claude obviously knows, but for your information, right now I'm working on the *sauce velouté* in this skillet." She was vigorously stirring some white viscous lumps with a wooden spoon.

"But it's just a veal stew, Jessie. Couldn't you have made everything in one pot?"

Jean-Claude sensed he was caught in a magnetic field between the two sisters.

"May I help you, Jessica?" he asked.

"Oh, that's *très gentil*. Do you know how to make a salad?"

"Yes," Jean-Claude replied. "That used to be my job at home. To have the salad ready when my mother came home from the clinic."

It took some moments till the girls' attention fixed upon Jean-Claude's activity. But gradually they both stopped working and just stared.

He had meticulously separated the lettuce leaves and immersed them one by one in water. Scrutinizing every leaf for imperfections, he placed those that passed on a towel, patting them with care.

After this, he reached on tiptoes for the olive oil and vinegar. Instants later he was scientifically measuring ingredients into a bowl. He then looked up at his enraptured audience and said:

"I need—I do not know the English for *de l'ail*."

"Jessie?" Paula asked her sister.

"We haven't had that word yet. I'll go look it up." And she sprinted toward the *Cassell's* in the living room. There were sounds of frantically ruffled pages and at last a triumphant shout of "Garlic!"

"Wow," said Paula to Jean-Claude. "Are you gonna be a French chef when you grow up?"

"No," the boy replied. "A doctor."

Jessie hurriedly reentered in search of garlic and a garlic press.

"When will they be home?" asked Paula.

"Well, Dad is jogging on the high school track

with birdbrain Bernie. He'll be just in time to be too late to do his share. Depending on the traffic, Mom should be here around seven."

"She'll be real excited when she sees you've made that blanket stew for her."

"*Blanquette*. I hope so. I—uh—Jean-Claude, could I ask you to—uh—taste the sauce?"

"Of course, Jessica." He walked over to the pot, dipped the wooden spoon in and brought it to his mouth.

"Mmm," he said softly, "very interesting."

"But is it good, is it *good*?" Jessica persisted.

"Superb," the little boy replied.

It was a triumph of international diplomacy.

13

"Do you see that fantastic kid? Isn't he great!
I can hardly believe he's my son!"

As the two fathers circled the Nanuet High
School track, Bernie kept touting his son's athletic
talents. At this moment, Davey Ackerman was on
the infield, scrimmaging with some of the older
soccer honchos.

"He's pretty good," Bob conceded.

"Good? Beckwith, the kid's fantastic. He's ambi-
dextrous. He's got all the moves. I mean, he's really
pro material. Don't you agree?"

"Uh—sure," said Bob, not wanting to interrupt
his friend's paternal fantasy. Besides, his legs still
bore some bruises from that collision with Bernie's
pride and joy.

"It's my business, after all," Bernie continued.
"The kid is everything I wasn't. Look at him slide
by those fullbacks!"

"Yeah," Bob answered noncommittally.

Bernie glanced at his friend and understood. His
tone of voice was sympathetic. "You know, women's
sports are getting to be really big too."

"Huh?"

"If you started your girls on a program now,

90

they'd have a chance for athletic scholarships. I could maybe even help."

"They hate sports, Bern."

"Whose fault is that?" replied the advocate of athletes, subtle accusation in his voice.

"They take ballet," Bob offered.

"Well, that's great prep for the high jump. And I think Jessie's gonna be tall. She could be a great high jumper, Beckwith."

"Why don't you tell her, Bern?"

"I don't know. For some reason she thinks I'm a clown. Doesn't she know I'm the top of my field?"

"Yeah. But I guess she's going through an anti-high-jump phase."

"Sit her down, Bob. Speak to her before it's too late."

They jogged along for another half mile, their increasingly labored breaths punctuated by Bernie's gasps of "Great" and "Fantastic" whenever Davey showed his style.

"Good workout," Bernie said when they reached the finish line and began to talk. "You should run during the year, too, Beckwith. I mean, how the hell do you stay so thin? You don't even play squash."

"I worry a lot," said Bob, and kept walking.

The soccer game had now disbanded and only Davey Ackerman remained, to practice kicking goals. Bernie could concentrate on other things. He turned to Bob.

"You seem down for some reason, Beckwith."

"It's nothing, Bern."

"Actually, when I think of it, Sheila looked a little down yesterday too. I mean, everything's okay with you guys, isn't it?"

Bob did not reply.

"Sorry. Stupid question, Bob. Nothing's ever wrong with you two."

Bob looked at him. "I gotta talk to someone, Bern."

"What am I here for, Beckwith?"

"Got five minutes?"

"Of course. Wanna sit on the stands?"

"Yeah."

They picked up their sweat clothes, wandered over to the flimsy wooden bleachers, climbed to the highest step and sat down.

"Okay, okay," said Bernie. "What the hell's the matter?"

Bob was too upset to start at the beginning.

"You know the French boy I brought over yesterday?"

"Yeah—the exchange kid. Nice-looking."

"He's mine."

"What do you mean?" Bernie was normally far from obtuse, but something visceral prevented him from understanding Bob's statement.

"He's my son," Bob repeated. Bernie's jaw dropped.

"Holy shit," he said. "You mean you've been cheating on Sheila all this time?"

"No, no. This was ten years ago. It wasn't even an 'affair.' I mean, more like a fling. The woman died last month. That was the first I ever heard about the boy."

"Are you really sure he's yours?"

"Yes."

"Holy shit," Bernie repeated, and then, "Hey—what was she like?"

"I don't remember."

"Christ, if I had a kid with a woman, I'd sure as hell remember what she looked like."

Bob started to explain that he hadn't known what

he was doing at the time. But this now sounded implausible, even to himself. Jean-Claude's very existence seemed to belie the most strenuous protestations of ignorance.

"Well?" Bernie asked again. "Was she good-looking?"

"I suppose so."

"Have you got a picture?"

Bob glared angrily at Bernie. "Will you be serious?"

"It was a reasonable question, Beckwith. If I ever cheated on Nancy—which I'd never have the guts to, 'cause it would kill her—it'd have to be with someone like Raquel Welch or better. And the least I'd do is save a picture."

Bob turned to him and said quietly, "Look at the boy. Her hair was darker, but she looked a lot like him."

It was at this moment that Bernie fully realized the significance of what Bob was telling him. "Holy shit," he mumbled. "*You.* My goddam role model. Christ, Sheila will never forgive you, will she?"

Bob glared at his best friend. Why the hell did he have to say a stupid thing like that, dammit?

And then something else dawned on Bernie.

"What the hell is he doing *here?*"

"He's got no other family. If we didn't take him, he'd already be in a state orphanage. A guy in France is trying to fix up something else. Sheila agreed to it."

"Christ, what a woman. Nancy would kick me *and* the kid out."

The track was silent now, and sunset cast long shadows on the field. The only sound was Davey Ackerman kicking his ball into the nets. Bernie was at a loss for words. He slowly shook his head and stared down through the wooden slats at the ground below. What could he say?

"Bob, I never dreamed a guy like you would screw around. I mean, you and Sheila were like those little figures on a wedding cake. What the hell made you do it?"

"I don't know, Bernie. It was ten years ago."

"In France?"

"Yeah."

There was a pause.

"Did you love her?"

Bob looked wounded. "Of course not," he shot back.

"I'm sorry," Bernie retorted. "I don't believe you. I don't believe a guy married to someone like Sheila would have an affair with a woman he didn't at least *think* he loved."

"I told you I don't remember," Bob said quietly. "The important thing is I don't know what to do now."

"Any idiot could tell that, Bob."

"What?"

"Get rid of the kid. Pronto. Fast. Amputate the relationship or your marriage will get gangrene. Am I making sense?"

"Yes."

"But I guess it's easier when you're not involved, huh?"

"Yes. Put yourself in my place."

"I couldn't. I've talked it over a million times."

"With whom?"

"With myself. You know how often I'm on the road—Miami, Vegas, L.A. I don't lack for opportunities. But I know Nancy trusts me, my kid looks up to me. I couldn't take the chance, Bob. I wouldn't. The only thing I've ever brought up to my hotel room is a bottle of Scotch. Hell, a client in Vegas once sent me up a fancy hooker. I mean, she was lust on wheels. When I told her I wasn't interested, she started wiggling those unbelievable tits and calling me all kinds of uncomplimentary names. I think I was drooling when I said no for the last time. But Christ, I was proud of myself. And you know something? I've never even confessed this part to Nancy—you know how I could hold out against those forty-inch boobs?"

"How?"

"I said to myself there's only one score in the marriage game. A thousand. No errors *ever*. Like Bob and Sheila. And I'm not the only one of your friends who thinks so, either. How's she taking it?"

"I think it's getting to her."

"I'll bet. That's why you've gotta ship that kid off now, Bob. You've got too much to lose."

"Hey, Dad!"

It was Davey Ackerman, shouting from the infield.

"Yeah?" Bernie shouted back.

"I'm ready to knock it off," called Davey.

"Okay, in a minute. Take two laps around first." Bernie then turned back to his friend.

"Hey, you know, Bob, I just thought of something ironic."

"What?"

"I mean, here you are a professor of statistics."

"So?"

"So you have one lousy affair in your whole life. For a few lousy days. And you get a kid as evidence. Christ, what are the odds of that happening to anybody?"

"Oh," said Bob bitterly, "about a billion to one."

14

"THE VEAL IS PERFECT, JESSIE."

"Do you really think so, Mom?"

"I think so too," said Bob, unasked. All during dinner he had been trying to read Sheila's face from across the table, but found it curiously indecipherable. They'd talk later, he reassured himself.

"What a nice surprise," Sheila added. "Did you make the salad dressing too?"

"Well . . ." said Jessie. Then she realized that if she did not attribute authorship, her sister would. "Uh—actually Jean-Claude made it."

"Really?" Sheila said, trying to seem pleased. "It's very good, Jean-Claude."

"Thank you," he answered shyly.

"He used to do it for his mom, every day," Paula added. "He can cook a lot of other stuff too."

"Oh," said Sheila, "that's nice." She was doing her best, dammit, and Bob wasn't helping at all.

"Anyone care for more *blanquette*?" asked Jessica.

At first there seemed no takers. Everybody's appetite was satisfied. But there was so much left.

"Uh—I would like some," said Jean-Claude. Jessie was delighted. Better to please one French palate than a dozen provincial know-nothings.

For dessert she had prepared Black Forest Cake à la Sara Lee. Provincial taste buds were suddenly reawakened.

"May we go watch television?" Paula asked her father.

"Can't you ever read a book?" said Bob, annoyed.

"Books are too scary," Paula protested.

"What are you talking about?" asked Bob.

"Jean-Claude has a schoolbook about *strangling*," Paula said, cringing in retrospect.

"What's this?" Bob asked the boy.

"I was reading the history of France. That is how Julius Caesar disposed of Vercingetorix the revolutionary."

"Ah," said Sheila. "That brings back memories of Mr. Hammond's Latin class. Do you enjoy history, Jean-Claude?"

"Not when it's sad. I was hoping Vercingetorix would win."

Bob smiled. "Why don't you go with the girls, Jean-Claude? It'll take your mind off strangling."

"Come on," said Paula, leaping from her chair.

The two girls scampered off. An instant later, the sound of sitcoms past was wafting in from the next room. But the French boy had not moved.

"Go on, Jean-Claude," said Bob. "It's a good way to practice your English."

"If you don't mind, Bob," he said politely, "I would prefer to read."

"Of course. More history?"

"Yes. I want to finish Julius Caesar." He got off his chair and started toward the stairway.

"You'll like what happens to him, Jean-Claude," Sheila called. "Brutus and Cassius get revenge for Vercingetorix."

"I know," he answered with a smile. "There is a picture."

When he had left the room, Sheila said something that totally astonished Bob.

"He's very cute."

They lingered over coffee in the dining room.

"How was Cambridge?" Bob inquired.

"Hot and tiring," she answered. "The Square was swarming with summer-school kids. . . ." Their dialogue was strangely awkward.

"See anyone?" Bob asked.

"Yes," she answered, and then, trying not to seem hostile, added, "Margo."

"How is she?" Bob asked, wondering if Sheila had confided in her friend as he had in his.

"The same."

"No new love?"

"Just the gallery. And I think she and Hal are not unhappy."

"That's hardly cause for cheering. Not being miserable isn't exactly my definition of an ideal marriage."

"Give Margo time. She's just learning."

"God knows she's had enough practice."

"Don't be snide."

"Sorry."

They finished their coffee in silence. Bob was now pretty sure she had told Margo. Then they began to talk again. Not really communicating, merely lobbing words over the net.

"Anything happen today?" Sheila asked.

"Nothing much. I jogged with Bernie. Oh, yeah— Louis Venarguès called."

"Oh. Has he made any progress?"

"Not yet. He just wanted to see if the boy was okay. They spoke for at least ten minutes."

"I think he's adjusted rather well, don't you?"

"Seems to have. Good kid," he said tentatively, "don't you think?"

"Yes," she said, "considering."

And then it suddenly occurred to Bob. *We are talking like unhappily married people.*

Even during vacation time, lights out was 10 P.M. for the Beckwith children. Jessie and Paula, all cooked out and viewed out, were more than willing to go to bed. After Sheila tucked them in, she joined Bob in their room.

"How're the kids?" he asked.

"In the arms of Morpheus. He's still reading, though."

"In bed?"

"Yes. His door was open."

"I missed you today," Bob whispered. She was tying her hair up, her back to him.

"Did you hear me, darling?"

"Yes," she said without turning.

"I—I don't want us to—grow distant, Sheila."

"No," she said, tonelessly.

"Will we?" he asked, a silent plea in his voice.

She turned around. "I hope not," she answered. And started for the door.

"Want a drink?" Bob asked, trying to anticipate her inclinations. "I'll go down and get it."

"No, thanks," she answered. "I just want to check on the boy."

And she left her husband alone with his uncertainties.

A soft light was still emanating from Jean-Claude's room. Sheila tiptoed quietly down the hallway and stopped at his door.

He had fallen asleep while reading. *Histoire Gé-*

nérale was still open across his chest. She looked down at him. There is nothing like a sleeping child to stir affection in the beholder.

And Sheila was by no means ill disposed toward him. During the hours of inner dialogue on the drive back to the Cape, she had become absolutely determined about one thing. The child was innocent. Whatever anger she might feel (and God, was she entitled to it) should be restricted to her husband. None of this was Jean-Claude's fault. None.

She watched him sleep. His brown hair had fallen across his brow. Should she brush it back? No, it might wake him. And he would be frightened suddenly to find himself in this strange environment so far from home. Now, asleep, he was just a nine-year-old child, breathing peacefully beneath his blanket and his book.

What if he should have a nightmare? Might he not wake and cry for someone now inexorably lost to him. Whom would he turn to?

You could come to me, she told him with her thoughts. I'd comfort you, Jean-Claude. I hope you haven't found me cold. I like you. Yes, I really do.

Up to now, her eyes had been focused on the little form in bed. It occurred to her to go and turn the light off next to him. Almost accidentally, her glance strayed to the night table. And then she froze. Her tenderness congealed.

Right by Jean-Claude's pillow was a picture in a silver frame. A photograph. Taken several months ago at most. It was Jean-Claude, sitting in an outdoor restaurant, smiling at a woman. A lovely raven-haired woman in a low-necked blouse, who was smiling back at him.

It was *she*. And she was beautiful. Very beautiful.

Evidently Jean-Claude only took the picture out at night.

Sheila turned away and left the light on.

"Was he asleep?" asked Bob.

"Yes," she answered. And her voice felt numb.

"Sheila," Bob said tenderly, "we'll work it out between us."

She could not respond.

"I love you, Sheila. Nothing's more important in the whole damn world."

She didn't answer.

She wanted to believe it. But no longer could.

15

THE NEXT MORNING BOB WOKE UP BEFORE SHEILA. Sunshine flooded the room. It was a glorious day. He looked over at his sleeping wife and wondered, How can I make her smile? He went downstairs to the kitchen, brewed coffee and brought it up to her.

"Oh, thank you," she said drowsily. (Almost smiling?)

He sat on the edge of the bed. "Hey, Sheila, it's absolutely gorgeous out. Why don't we take a little trip to Provincetown?"

"The two of us?"

"Everybody."

Damn. The instant he'd replied, Bob realized he had blown a unique opportunity.

Still, once they arrived in the quaint fishing village/artist colony/tourist trap, his spirits again lifted. They all seemed happy to be there. Narrow Commercial Street (an apt name, Bob had always thought) was teeming with tourists in loud summer shirts and even louder sunburns. At the first appropriate shop, Jessica insisted upon buying a pair of eminently garish pink sunglasses.

"Wow," said Paula. "Could I get a pair like that too?"

"Absolutely not," Bob insisted. "She looks like Dracula's daughter."

"I resent that," said Sheila, with a twinkle of humor in her voice.

"Ho ho, Father," said Jessica, "you're really out of it. It so happens that these are very chic in Europe. Right, Jean-Claude?"

"They are interesting," the boy conceded, "but I do not think I have seen them before."

"Well, you will," said Jessica, and wafted ahead to study the psychedelic shopwindows.

Later, they all climbed up to the Pilgrim Monument, looked briefly with the requisite reverence and started down again. The two girls walked slightly ahead with Sheila, stopping now and then to peer at antiques. Jean-Claude remained at Bob's side. Touched by this, Bob began to discourse like a Baedeker, pointing out the sights they passed. All the while he had been studying a contemporary attraction just ahead of them.

"See that chick in the white shorts? She's got the nicest legs we've seen all day."

Just then the leggy beauty—Sheila Beckwith—turned and smiled at them. Had she heard Bob? He hoped so.

By midafternoon, they were at MacMillan Wharf, where they all ate quahogs.

"We say it ko-hogs," Paula told the visitor, who was having difficulty pronouncing the name of the clams he was eating.

Bob then bought everybody soft ice cream, and they strolled out on the pier to watch the fishermen unload the day's catch. For Jean-Claude this was the best part of the day. But something puzzled him.

"Are they speaking Spanish?" he inquired.

"Portuguese," said Sheila. "Most of the fisher-men here came from Portugal."

When they had walked back to the car and were climbing in, Jean-Claude remarked, "I like this place. It reminds me of my home."

Minutes later, they were cruising along the ocean on Route 6A. Bob was pleased. The excursion had been a success. Not only were the kids elated, but even Sheila seemed to have enjoyed herself. He glanced at his watch. It was nearly five o'clock.

"Hey, guys," he said, "I've got a great idea."

"What?" asked Paula, always eager to expand her horizons.

"Well, I promised to meet Uncle Bernie at the track about now. Why don't we all go?"

"Negative," was Jessie's immediate and dour reply. "I don't need to jog away my menopause just yet."

Bob sighed. Why do I even try with her? he thought.

He then addressed his ally. "Want to come, Paula?"

"Gee, Dad, I'm kinda tired. Maybe tomorrow."

Two strikes. Somewhat timidly, he asked his wife. "Sheila?"

"I don't think so, Bob," she said gently, "but we could drop you off at the track and Bernie could give you a lift home."

"Okay," he said, now resigned to the loneliness of the long-distance jogger. They drove for several miles without further conversation. Then Jean-Claude spoke.

"May I come, please?" he asked.

Bob was delighted. "You mean you'd like to run?"

"No," the boy replied, "but I would like to watch you."

Bernie was warming up, his eyes constantly on the infield, where Davey was once again outclassing the high school soccer stars. Then he noticed his friend appear in the distance.

"Ho, Beckwith!" he call without interrupting his jumping jacks. "Ho—uh—kid!"

Not that Bernie had a feeble memory. He could quote every major league batting average since the game began. But the sight of Bob's . . . problem actually walking toward him rendered him momentarily speechless. He was, to put it simply, freaked out.

"Hiya, Bern."

"Hello, Mr. Ackerman," said Jean-Claude.

"Hi. Uh—how's it hanging, kid? You gonna run with us?"

"No, I will just wait for Bob."

"Sports are really crucial for growing boys," stated Bernie, and then turned to indicate the action on the field. "Lookit Davey. He's gonna grow up to be a regular Tarzan."

"Maybe Jean-Claude doesn't want to swing from trees," Bob interposed. "C'mon, Bern, let's get on the road."

"Okay. See ya—uh—Jean-Claude."

The men chugged off. The boy walked to the stands, climbed to the fourth tier, where he had a good view of the entire track, and sat down.

"So, Beckwith?" whispered Bernie as soon as they were on the curve.

"So what?"

"So when's he leaving?"

"I told you, Bern. Sheila agreed to a month's visit."

"Okay, okay. Just remember, I warned you that what a wife thinks and what she says don't always match."

"Let's just run, huh?"

Bob picked up the pace, hoping to tire his partner into silence.

"That reminds me," Bernie puffed. "You know what you've told me is buried in the Fort Knox of my brain. The whole Gestapo couldn't get it out of me. But—"

"But what?"

"I'd really like to tell Nance. I mean, husbands and wives shouldn't have secrets from each other."

Bob did not respond.

"Beckwith, I swear, Nancy's the soul of honor. The epitome of discretion. Besides, she'll notice I'm holding out on her. I mean, God knows what she'll think it is."

"She'd never guess," Bob said wryly.

"That's just the point. Please, Beckwith, Nance'll be discreet. I swear on my clients' lives."

The pressure was too great.

"Okay, Bern," he sighed, "but not too many details, huh?"

"Don't sweat. Just the essential wild fact—if you know what I mean."

"Yeah. When'll you tell her?"

Three strides later, Bernie answered sheepishly, "Last night."

The high school soccer studs began to disband, bidding farewell to Davey Ackerman. Since yesterday he'd practiced kicking goals, today he'd do a little work on dribbling. And so he began to trot around the perimeter of the field, nudging the ball before him with alternating feet.

When he reached the stands, he noticed Jessica

Beckwith's foreign guest seated by himself. He trapped the ball under his foot, stopped short, and pivoted toward the stands.

"Hey!" he called.

"Yes?" Jean-Claude replied.

"You the French kid staying at the Beckwiths?"

"Yes."

"How come you're always just sitting around, huh?"

Jean-Claude shrugged.

"What is wrong with that?" he asked. He vaguely sensed that he was being challenged to something.

"How come you're always with Jessica Beckwith, huh?" Davey's tone was now distinctly belligerent.

"Uh—I am her guest. She is my friend." Jean-Claude was not quite sure how to respond. He was growing uneasy.

"She's *my* girl, Frenchie, do you understand that? *My* girl," Davey insisted, thumbing his expanded chest for emphasis.

"My name is not Frenchie," the boy said quietly.

Ahh, thought Davey, I've found a sore point.

"Yeah? Well, I'll call you whatever the hell I want, whenever the hell I want, how many times I want—plus ten more. Frenchie, Frenchie, Frenchie . . ."

Davey was standing there, his right foot on the soccer ball, his right hand making a sophisticated gesture in conjunction with his nose.

Jean-Claude stood up.

Davey inhaled and drew himself to his full height, which was appreciably greater than the younger boy's.

"Gonna try something, Frenchie?" he taunted.

Jean-Claude slowly descended from the stands and approached Davey, whose game plan was now to stand as tall as possible, emanating strength, thus striking fear into his smaller opponent.

"My name is Jean-Claude Guérin," the boy said quietly, still walking slowly toward him.

"And I say it's Frenchie. Sissy Frenchie Fruitcake."

Jean-Claude was now less than a foot away. Davey towered over him. "Frenchie Fruitcake," Davey repeated, grinning.

And then Jean-Claude kicked.

Not Davey, but the ball beneath his foot. Davey fell back onto his behind.

From far off, his departing soccer buddies caught sight of the young superstar's tumble and began to laugh. Davey rose from the ground, infuriated.

He started toward Jean-Claude, who backed up, still keeping the ball in control.

"My name is Jean-Claude," he repeated.

Davey lunged to kick the ball away. Jean-Claude deftly tapped it out of his reach.

Now the French boy dribbled toward midfield. Davey gave chase. He sprinted and lunged. Jean-Claude feinted and dodged. Davey could not get anywhere near the ball. The team guys now began to whistle and applaud. They had never seen such ball handling by so young a kid. They hadn't learned in school that European children begin kicking as soon as they begin walking.

The hoots and jeers now became audible even to the tired joggers on the far side of the field. Bernie was the first to notice. He could not believe his eyes.

"Holy shit!" he remarked. "The kid's an athlete!"

At first Bob did not bother to look up, assuming it was yet another of Bernie's panegyrics to his son. Then he did.

And he saw Jean-Claude feinting as Davey Ackerman tackled for the ball—and this time landed face down in the dust.

He felt a shiver. My God, he thought, *my son's* fantastic! He stopped running to watch.

"Bravo, Jean-Claude!" he shouted. "*Bien joué, bien joué!*"

"Beckwith," Bernie said quietly, "you've gotta get rid of that kid before it's too late."

"What the hell do you mean, 'too late'?"

"Before you fall in love with him."

16

How was your run?" Sheila asked.

"Not bad," said Bob.

"Did you have a good time, Jean-Claude?"

"Yes, thank you."

"He played some soccer," Bob added, his voice unable to conceal his pride. "You should have seen him. He's really very good."

Jean-Claude beamed. Bob saw him in the corner of his eye and felt a further joy that his words of praise had so pleased the boy.

"How about washing up for dinner, Jean-Claude?"

"Okay, Bob," he said, and skipped out of the kitchen.

Bob kissed Sheila on the cheek. "Dinner smells great. What is it?"

"Just odds and ends."

"Can I help?"

"Yes. Peel some potatoes."

"Sure." He was happy to be doing something with her again—even if it was only KP. He put on an apron and began to peel.

One potato later, Sheila mentioned, "Evelyn called."

"To inquire if you're having a good time?"

"No. To ask if I could come to Cambridge tomorrow."

"She's got a lot of nerve. I sure as hell hope you told her where to go."

"She pleaded, actually. It's pretty important."

"Honey, Evelyn Unger is a workaholic and a slave driver. The Harvard Press is *not* the *New York Times*. What couldn't possibly wait three weeks?"

"Gavin Wilson," she replied.

"Isn't he in Washington teaching the National Security Council how to attack Massachusetts?"

"Yes. But he'll be in Cambridge tomorrow. Only tomorrow."

"What does that have to do with you?"

"He's a big star on our backlist. And Evelyn wants to cash in on his new visibility and reissue his books."

"I thought university presses weren't supposed to be venal. Besides, Wilson's foreign policy stuff is old hat."

"Which is why Evelyn wants me to meet with him. She wants to convince him to do some revisions and updating."

"And for this you have to sacrifice a chunk of your vacation?"

She looked at him and said quietly, "I'm flattered to be asked, Bob."

He understood. Or at least thought he did. At this delicate moment she wanted some objective reaffirmation of her worth. He should be glad for her.

"Yeah," he said after another potato, "it is flattering, isn't it? Well, haven't I always said you were the best damn editor they had? I say it's about time they acknowledged it."

"And I say keep peeling," she replied cheerfully.

* * *

Bob had made a fire, and they were sitting peacefully, listening to the music of the waves.

"Hey," he said as spontaneously as possible. "I've got an idea."

"What's that?" she asked.

"Why don't we drive up to Cambridge together?"

"What about the kids?" Ah, thought Bob optimistically, she's not averse.

"We could get Susie Ryder to sleep over."

"Sleep over?" He had tipped his hand a bit.

"Well, I thought we might give ourselves a break and stay over at the Lexington house. Just the two of us."

His eyes were saying, Come on, Sheila, we both need this.

"It's a bit impractical," she replied.

"Okay, then let's just go up, you have your meeting, I'll buy some records at the Coop, we can have an early dinner and come back."

Please, Sheila, he was thinking. Please see how badly I want to splice the broken wires of our relationship.

She mulled it over.

"Not this time, Bob," she said at last.

Well, at least it was a conditional rejection. "Not this time" had an implicit corollary of perhaps another time.

She stood up.

"I'd better get a good night's sleep," she said. And before he could rise to join her, she walked over to his chair, put her arm near his head, and whispered, "Thanks for asking."

Then she kissed him lightly on the forehead and started to the stairs.

A small gesture. But it was the best thing that had happened to him in weeks.

17

H_I, S_{HEILA}," CALLED M_{AUREEN} THE RECEPTION-
ist. "He's in Evelyn's office. Lucky you."

Funny, thought Sheila, as she started down the
corridor toward the editorial department. Maureen's
usually blasé, accustomed to the likes of Kissinger
and Galbraith parading by.

When she turned the corner, she saw him having
coffee with Evelyn at her desk. He was long and
lanky, with graying hair and square tortoise-shell
glasses. He was wearing jeans and a T-shirt reading
GO BOSTON RED SOX! She was somewhat startled, for
she had prepared herself to meet a three-piece suit
(the Washington influence) with a cultured English accent (the Oxford influence).

He stood up as she approached. He was very tall.
Evelyn introduced them.

"Gavin, this is Sheila Beckwith, our number one
editor."

"How do you do," said Wilson. (At least the
accent was still there.) "I understand you've had to
interrupt your holiday on my account. I'm terribly
sorry."

"On the contrary, I'm happy to have the chance
of working with you, Dr. Wilson."

"Gavin, please. And may I call you Sheila?"

"Of course. I know you're on a tight schedule. Would you like to come right to my office and begin?"

He smiled and turned to Evelyn. "You didn't exaggerate—she's a harsh taskmaster." And then, turning to Sheila, "May I get you a coffee en route?"

"Please," said Sheila. "White, no sugar."

By the time he entered her office, Sheila had already placed all three of his books on her desk and was spreading out some sheets of yellow paper.

He placed the containers of coffee on the corner of the desk and then sat down across from her.

"Thank you," she said. And then, to break the ice, asked, "Do you miss Cambridge at all?"

"Yes, I do. Though Washington does have its compensations. At Harvard one has one's share of glory, but working at the White House, there is that scintilla of power. Which I confess I quite enjoy."

"I admire your candor."

"In any case, if and when this administration's voted out, I do hope I'll be asked back here. If they'll welcome a prodigal son."

"Oh, they will," smiled Sheila, "especially since your books will have been reissued and updated."

"Well, I can see I'm being buttered up to do serious revisions," he said. "But to speak with that same candor you approve of, I was really thinking along the lines of, you know, 'Preface to the second edition' sort of thing. And then I could plead Washington pressures for not being able to revamp the whole business."

"Well, in that case, you don't need me," Sheila replied pleasantly but firmly, "and I don't think the Press would reissue your books with nothing but cosmetic changes."

Wilson shifted a bit uneasily in his chair, took a sip of coffee and then looked at Sheila.

"You're not too bad in the candor department, either." He smiled. "Uh—what sort of things did *you* have in mind?"

"Well, these are only first impressions. I've only been able to skim the books since Evelyn called me. But take *The Re-Emergence of Postwar Germany*. It was the best thing published in its time. It's not your fault that it came out just before Brandt began his *Ostpolitik*."

He affected a slight frown. "Mmm," he said. "I'm afraid you're right. Anything else?"

"Yes, I'm sorry. But there are a lot of things we'd have to go over in detail. Still, if I were you, I'd take the time. Now that you're in the papers a little more than the average Harvard professor, some of your academic colleagues—which is to say everybody who didn't get appointed to the Security Council—will start trying to punch holes in your scholarship."

He smiled broadly. "How do you know university politics so well?"

"My husband's a professor at MIT."

"Really? What's his field?"

"Statistics."

"Oh, a real brain. I'm always self-conscious when I meet that sort of mind. I can barely add a column of figures."

"Neither can Bob." Sheila smiled. "That's my job at the end of every month."

"Oh," said Gavin Wilson. "Then my admiration for you knows no bounds."

And now his smile did not seem to be solely for Sheila's arithmetical ability.

In any case, considering the ice fairly well broken, Sheila got back to business.

"So you can see you've got even more at stake in these revisions than we do."

"Yes, but if I understand your drift, you're asking for an enormous amount of work."

She nodded. "But your editor is willing to do her share."

"That's a genuine inducement," said Wilson, "so let's get on with it. I'll try not to be too depressed."

"May I continue to be frank?"

"By all means be brutal. Rather you than the critics. Besides, I have a resilient ego."

"Well," Sheila continued, "*Anglo-American Relations* needs an updated epilogue, but otherwise it's in fine shape."

"Bloody lucky. Especially since that one got me my Harvard appointment. How about my Common Market thing?"

"Well," Sheila answered slowly, searching for tactful words, "even as we speak, that picture's changing. And you did make occasional predictions that have proved—well—somewhat off target."

"Dead wrong, you mean. Like there'd never be a European parliament and all that. I'd make a pretty bad clairvoyant, wouldn't I?" He said it all with good humor, and then added, "Now I have a rather serious question."

"Yes?"

"What do you hear about a restaurant called Harvest?"

"Uh—it's quite good."

"Let's go then, shall we?"

Margo would doubtless be at her daily corner table. But what the hell—this was business, wasn't it?

*　　*　　*

Gavin dressed for lunch. Which is to say he put a dungaree jacket over his Red Sox T-shirt. When they got to the restaurant, it was rather late. Most people were having coffee and dessert—and Margo seemed to have left.

It was July, and Cambridge was an oven. So they ordered iced tea instead of an apéritif. Facing a long afternoon of editorial negotiations, they restricted their luncheon conversation to small talk.

"What is your husband working on at the moment?"

"Nothing serious. Our month at the Cape is strictly for reading paperbacks."

"Ah, a well-adjusted academic. Not too compulsive. Wish I could resist the *furor scribendi*. But I'm still driven to publish. Do you have any children?"

This most innocuous of social queries jolted her out of the temporary amnesia she was enjoying.

"Uh—yes," she replied after a split second. "Two girls, nine and twelve. You?"

"Two. Quite grown up. My son's reading medicine at Oxford, Gemma's still at home with my ex-wife. But she'll be starting some sort of comparative literature thing at East Anglia this fall. I don't think they miss their father much, but I'm afraid I do them."

"You must get over there for the State Department now and then, don't you?"

"Oh, the odd forty-eight-hour whirlwind. I call them, but they're always too busy with something or other. I think my wife's propaganda has done its work."

"Are you on very bad terms—or shouldn't I ask?"

"Not at all. Yes, we are on extremely bad terms. She's never forgiven me for joining the British brain drain. Not that she has anything against America—

she's never been here. But she objects to it in principle. So, having made me choose between her and Harvard—never expecting I would take the latter—she's been a bit ill-disposed towards me ever since. I'm still fond of her, if that counts for anything. And I miss the children. Oh—but I'm repeating myself. Do forgive me for babbling on about boring domestic matters."

He looked at her. She did not seem bored, but she was a very bright, attractive woman, and he was anxious to make a good impression.

"You're not boring me at all," she answered, genuinely happy to be discussing someone else's domestic problems. And then she asked him, "Are you bitter?"

He seemed unprepared for her question. "Do I seem bitter?" he asked.

"No, of course not," she said quickly, "and it was impolite of me to ask."

"Not at all," he protested. "It was just unnecessary."

Now she was surprised. "I don't understand," she said.

"You're perspicacious enough to have noticed without asking. You could tell before my monologue was halfway through that my pride was—shall we say—sprained. Why else would I have told you when we could have been discussing things of interest to us both?"

Sheila did not know what to say. She was curiously flattered. She had never considered herself perceptive about anyone except Bob and the children. But Gavin was obviously trying to flatter her. After all, he had a reputation for suavity.

As she was reaching for the credit cards in her purse, he put his hand on hers.

"Just what do you think you're doing?" he asked.

"Paying the check," she replied. "This was Harvard Press business."

"Please, I insist. All we did was talk about my domestic sorrows."

"No. I like to use my expense account. It makes me feel important."

She removed her hand, found her credit card, signaled the waiter and settled the bill.

"Thank you, Sheila," he smiled. "Are you always this persuasive?"

"Only when it comes to my job," she smiled back.

By five-thirty they had worked their way painstakingly through four chapters, marking in the margins where revisions or at least rechecking would be necessary. By now Sheila was getting tired.

"You'll have to excuse me, Gavin," she said, barely suppressing a yawn, "but I've got a long drive back to the Cape. I can go through the rest of the chapters, make Xeroxes of the pages that need revision, and send them on to you in Washington. . . ."

He looked up from his bifocals and asked, "Must you?"

She nodded. "I've got a family waiting. Anyway, the important thing is that we've met and agree on the changes."

"Yes," Gavin said. "I'm very glad we've met."

She started to gather her papers and put them into her zipper case.

"Sheila?" He was now standing, looking down at her. "Since the Press so graciously invited me to lunch, I'd like to reciprocate by asking you to dinner."

She looked up at him. What had increasingly

impressed her all afternoon was not his good looks, but his manner. Patient and good-humored. Irony without cynicism.

"I really should be getting back," she protested in a way she hoped would not sound too definitive. "They expect me."

"Couldn't you ring them? After all, we'd be able to discuss more revisions."

She paused for a moment. What was her hurry to return to the minefield that she once called home?

"Well, actually, I might be able to stay over with a friend in Cambridge."

"Splendid. You ring them from here, and I'll nip into Evelyn's office and book a table."

As soon as she was alone, she dialed Margo at the gallery.

"Darling—are you in Cambridge again? Have things exploded at the Cape?"

"No. I had to do some work at the Press. In fact, if you don't mind, I may call you later and ask if I can stay over."

"Oh, that's wonderful. Hal's off fishing with his children. All they probably catch is the tuna I packed for them. That means we can have a midnight party like the old days in Joss. Shall we meet for dinner?"

"Uh—no. I've got a few more hours of work."

"Then you definitely must stay. I'll chill some wine. Oh, this'll be fun."

Then she called Bob and told him. He did not conceal his disappointment.

"What about the kids?" he asked plaintively.

"You're there," she replied. "They can manage without me for one night."

"I can't manage without you," he answered.

*　　*　　*

The place was dimly lit, the checkered tables crowded with an *insalata mista* of young college couples and noisy Italian families.

They relaxed easily into friendly conversation.

"You seem to enjoy your work," Gavin remarked.

"I do," Sheila replied.

"Well, you're bloody good at it. I mean, it's a rare editor who doesn't hide behind coy euphemisms when they think a paragraph is total rubbish."

"Tell me about Washington," she said.

"Tell me more about you," he countered.

"I've told you everything, really. My life's pretty conventional compared to yours."

Again she had deliberately shifted the topic back to him. I'm not *that* fascinating, he told himself. Still it was refreshing to encounter someone who could actually resist talking about themselves.

"Do you see the President much?" she asked.

"There's no such person. With rare exceptions, the Oval Office is occupied by well-tailored actors who read scripts written for them by a team of writers—of whom I am one. Actually the present incumbent is more like that robot chap in *Star Wars*."

"You're being naughty," she smiled.

"Oh, I thought I was being irreverently charming."

"You were that too. In fact, you're everything the columns say you are."

"Am I? I never read the things."

"Neither do I," said Sheila, "but my staff clip them and put them on my desk."

He looked straight into her mischievous green eyes and said, "Touché." And added, "Perhaps I need a new scriptwriter."

"No," she answered. "Just an editor." Almost as she said it, she realized the embarrassing ambiguity, and added as quickly as possible, "I'd love to hear more about our robot President."

"No," he said emphatically. "You can read Jack Anderson for that. Tell me about your other authors. Are they all as vain as I?"

At least this was a topic that did not make her uneasy.

"I don't usually have much personal contact with them. Most of our editing is done by mail."

"Lucky me," he said warmly.

The ambiguity of *his* remark made her too shy to speak.

Gavin gazed at Sheila's face across the candles, wondering why this lovely woman seemed—despite her playful outward manner—to emanate such sadness.

"You know, you're extremely attractive, Sheila," he said.

She tried desperately to look happily married.

"Do you think I'm just flattering you?" he asked.

"Yes," she said.

"Don't believe everything you read. I'm not playing the devious roué."

"I never thought so," she replied, convincing neither of them.

"Good," he said. "I'm glad. That means you'll accept my invitation for a nightcap without any superfluous qualms."

"No, really, I can't. My friends are expecting me."

"The Sheraton Commander's midway between there and here."

His hotel. God, was he predictable. And so persistent. What a line! Did he ever actually succeed with it?

Of course he did. Because in other circumstances he might well succeed in making her believe she was attractive and desirable. How ironic that it happened now, when she was at the very nadir of her confidence as a woman.

"Sheila?" Gavin repeated, still awaiting her response.

"Uh—I would love to . . ."

"Fine."

"But really I'm exhausted. I wouldn't be much fun." He could construe that in accordance with the subtext of his own intention.

"Some other time then," he said good-naturedly, and rose to help her from her chair.

They drove in silence (past the Commander) to the Harvard Press. He waited while she got into her car.

"Thank you, Gavin," Sheila said.

And he replied, "I can't tell you how much I look forward to working with you."

18

Ah! You weren't working overtime. You had a date."

"I had dinner with an *author*, Margo."

"I don't care if he was a trapeze artist. He was a man and you were out with him. By my definition, that's a date. Now tell me *everything*."

As she sat down on the couch, Sheila realized that this was the first time in her life that she actually *wanted* to share her intimate thoughts with Margo.

"May I have a glass of that wine," she said.

Margo poured her some. "Now let's hear everything. Oh, isn't this just like the Vassar days?"

Was it? Things were much more frivolous then. And much less married.

"Well . . ." Sheila began with the innocuous: "Evelyn asked me to come up today for a special rush project. We're reissuing three of Gavin Wilson's books."

"That's rather on the ball for them," offered Margo. "He's certainly a rising star. But couldn't it have waited till the end of your holiday?"

"Not really. Gavin was only up in Cambridge for the day."

"Gavin?" Margo grinned. "We're already on a first-name basis, are we?"

"Come on, Margo—it's just work."

"Of course," she answered sarcastically. "Is he as handsome as his photographs?"

"I suppose so," Sheila answered noncommittally.

"Does he have an English accent?"

"Well, he does come from England."

"English accents are seductive, don't you think?"

"They can be."

Sheila would have preferred simply to chronicle the events. But Margo's radar was picking up the unspoken signals.

"Did he like you?"

Sheila paused.

"Well, he thinks I'm a good editor."

"Editor shmeditor. Where did he take you for dinner?"

"La Groceria in Central Square."

"Ah, candlelight—very romantic. And of course you only discussed revisions?"

"Certainly."

"Liar."

"Well, it's normal to chat about other things too."

"Of course," said Margo. "And when did he make his pass?"

"What?"

"Come on, Sheil. He's gorgeous, he's eligible, and he's notorious."

"But I'm—"

"And you're a *very* pretty lady."

"I was about to say I'm married."

Margo looked at her with eyebrow raised. "And the world is round," she stated, "none of which has anything to do with Gavin Wilson."

Sheila took another sip and said, "This is good wine."

"Ah, so I'm *right*. Now tell me what he said and I'll tell you what he meant."

"The whole evening?"

"No, you idiot. Just the postprandial pitch."

"There was none. He drove me to my car. That's all."

"Silently? No dialogue?"

Sheila paused. Now she had misgivings about saying any more to Margo.

"Well, he did ask me for a drink. I don't think it was anything."

Margo's eyes widened. "A drink? *Where?*"

"At his hotel."

"I would say that was a pretty definitive pass, wouldn't you?"

"Maybe," Sheila conceded, "I guess so."

"Then what the hell are you doing *here?*"

"That sort of thing is hardly my lifestyle," Sheila answered.

Margo got up and sat next to her on the couch.

"Listen lovey," she said quietly, taking Sheila's hand, "you've always been the perfect wife and you've just had your ego flattened with a steam roller. Doesn't it make you feel good to find out that a really super guy thinks you're terrific?"

"I . . . I was sort of flattered, yes."

"Then I repeat my question—what on earth are you doing here?"

"Margo, I've been through enough humiliation. I don't have to be some English Casanova's little nocturnal distraction."

"Is that all you think he wants?"

"It doesn't matter, Margo. Because despite this wretched mess, I still love Bob and I don't want my marriage to suffer any more than it has."

"What makes you so sure your marriage would suffer?"

Sheila tried to read Margo's intention from her face. She seemed genuinely concerned. This was not the pseudo-sophisticate of Josselyn Hall, the advocate of Free Love who had remained a virgin till her wedding day. This was someone who was trying to tell a friend she really cared for that, sadly, nothing in life was perfect. A fact that Sheila evidently had been slow to learn.

"Look, Sheil," Margo continued, "this has nothing to do with revenge or getting back at Bob. He doesn't ever have to know. . . ."

"But he loves me," Sheila murmured, "and he's really been making such an effort."

Margo looked at her wounded friend. What more could she say without alienating her?

One more thing.

"What about the gorgeous French doctor?"

This really hurt.

"Damn," said Sheila. Her teeth were clenched in anger. She did not really wish to think about the beauty of the late Nicole Guérin.

The two women sat in silence for a moment. Finally Margo asked, "How exactly did you leave it with Gavin?"

"I just told him I was tired."

"Oh? So you didn't slam the door and bolt it, did you?"

"No is no."

"Weren't you the slightest bit tempted?"

What was the point of denying it now?

"Margo, where could it lead?"

"Nowhere, probably. But it might just make you a little less unhappy. Anyway, you'll never know unless you follow it up."

Sheila wanted to end—or at least postpone—further discussion.

"Look," she said, "we'll be working on his books in the next couple of months. There'll be plenty of time to—"

"No," said Margo softly but firmly, "call him *now*."

"What?"

"It's only 10:20; call him now. Before you lose your nerve."

"What could I say? It's so embarrassing."

"Just tell him you had a lovely evening. Let him make the next move. At the worst you'll have kept the door open."

Sheila took a deep breath. "This is wrong," she said aloud to herself.

"Where's he staying?" Margo asked.

"The Sheraton Commander."

In an instant, Margo was leafing through the phonebook. She found the number, scratched it on a piece of paper, and handed it to Sheila.

"Come on honey, call," she said.

"I can't."

"Then I will."

"Please, Margo."

"All right, Sheila, it's your life. I don't want to play Mephistopheles. Be unhappy on your own terms." She started to scrunch the paper into a ball. Then Sheila blurted out.

"Wait. I—I'll do it."

Her fingers trembled slightly as she pressed the buttons on the telephone.

"Sheraton Commander. Good evening."

"Uh—" Sheila's voice was suddenly dry and slightly hoarse. "Uh—may I speak to . . . Gavin Wilson, please?"

"Ringin' Dr. Wilson's room. . . ."

Sheila gave an anguished look at Margo, who nodded to assure her she was doing the right thing.

The next moments seemed endless. Then the operator returned to the line.

"No answer in Dr. Wilson's room. Would you like to leave a message, dear?"

"Uh—no, thank you." Sheila let the receiver slide from her hand back onto the phone.

Thank God.

19

J EAN-CLAUDE WAS SEATED IN HIS USUAL SPOT ON THE beach. Today studying *Initiation à la Géographie*. He had been there since early morning, having risen before the rest of the family and, in Sheila's absence, made coffee, drunk a cup and left the rest for Bob.

Jessica appeared on the quiet seashore some time later, carrying her paperback of *Anna Karenina* (with the new television-series cover), and walked to a dune far down the beach. They sat like bookends for two hundred yards of silent sand and driftwood.

The sun was nearing its meridian when an unwelcome shadow cut off Jessie's reading light.

"Whatcha doing, Jess?"

She looked up. It was that philistine Davey Ackerman.

"Reading," she replied. "And I'd be grateful if you'd quit blocking my sun."

"I got something to tell you, Jess," he said.

"It couldn't be anything I could possibly want to hear. Buzz off."

"What'll you do if I tell you a secret? If it's good, will you like me more?"

"It'd have to be a really great secret."

"This one'll really shake you up."

"Oh, yeah?"

"Yeah."

She closed her *Anna Karenina* and looked at Davey with her customary disdain. "What?" she said.

"Walk with me to the cove."

"Why?"

"Because it's gotta be in private, Jess. Where no one can even see us. I could get killed if anyone found out."

The thought of a man risking his life just to impart something to her piqued Jessie's interest. She stood up.

"Okay," she said, brushing the sand off her shorts. "This better be worth it."

They walked till they had rounded a dune in the cove and were absolutely invisible save for the low-flying gulls.

"Well?" asked Jessica impatiently.

"Okay, listen," he said, taking a deep breath to summon up his courage. "I heard my parents talking last night, see?"

"Yeah?"

"They were whispering kind of loud. About your parents . . ."

Jessie grew slightly anxious. She had lately noticed a slight coolness between Bob and Sheila, but had refused to ascribe any importance to it. Not them, she had told herself. They're happy.

"What about my parents?" she asked, unconsciously biting her nail.

"Well, it was about the French kid, actually."

"What?"

"He's your father's."

"What are you talking about?" demanded Jessie, frightened that she might have understood.

"He's your father's kid. Your father is his father," Davey blurted nervously. "You get it?"

"You're a filthy liar."

"No, I swear. He is. I heard my parents. I mean, they're so freaked you can't imagine."

"Davey, you're a dirty little bastard!" Jessie shouted, on the verge of tears.

"Cool it, Jess," he pleaded. Her unexpected tantrum was upsetting him. He had hoped for something more like gratitude. But she turned away.

"Come back," he shouted.

She had started running down the beach.

"What was he like, Mom?" Paula asked, as Sheila unpacked her briefcase, piling Gavin Wilson's three books on her desk.

"Nice," she replied. "Actually I expected him to be a little conceited, but he wasn't." She was careful to place the volumes with the front covers facing upward. So Gavin's photograph would not stare up to remind her of what almost happened yesterday.

"What did you have for dinner last night?" she asked, hoping her daughter would not notice the blatant shift of subject.

"We had fun."

"And what else?"

"Dad took us out for pizza. It was fun," and then, realizing her lapse in tact, she added, "Of course, it woulda been better if you were there too, Mom."

"Thanks." Sheila laughed and kissed her on the forehead. Just then the front door slammed.

"Mom, where are you?" Jessie shouted.

"In here, Jess. I just got back this instant—"

Jessica entered the room, her face flushed and sweating.

"What's the matter, honey?" Sheila asked.

"Is it true?" Jessie demanded, her voice quavering.

"What?"

"Is it true about Daddy?"

"Uh—I don't know, Jessie." At least I hope I don't, she thought.

"Then it *is* true. I can see it on your face."

"What's going on?" inquired Paula, anxious to participate in the family crisis.

Jessie turned to Paula. "Davey told me that Jean-Claude is Daddy's *son!*"

"What? You're crazy!"

Paula was wide-eyed. She could not quite fathom what she was hearing but vaguely sensed that it was terrible.

"Please," said Sheila, frantically trying to preserve all of their sanity, "let me try to explain. . . ."

Jessie turned angrily on her mother.

"First admit it's true. Tell me Dad is really Jean-Claude's—" She couldn't bring herself to say the word.

"Yes," Sheila said quietly, "it's true."

Now Paula began to cry.

"No." She shook her head. "It's some big lie. He's our daddy. He's *ours!*"

Jessie exploded at her sister.

"Don't you understand, you little idiot? He had an affair with Jean-Claude's mother."

"What's an 'affair'?" said Paula, wanting desperately not to understand.

"He went to bed with her and made a baby," Jessie shouted.

Paula looked helplessly at her mother.

"Is Daddy gonna leave us?" she asked, voicing her deepest fears.

Sheila took the two frightened girls in her arms. "It'll be all right," she murmured, hoping to make herself believe it.

"How could you let him come here," Jessie sobbed, "into our house?"

Just then the front door slammed again. They froze. And Jean-Claude, book in hand, walked into the room.

"Good afternoon," he smiled. He was especially happy to see Sheila again.

"He's *our* daddy," Paula exploded at him. "He's ours, he's ours!"

Jean-Claude was confused.

"What do you mean, Paula?" he asked.

"Our daddy is your father, and you want to take him away," she screamed.

"But no—" Jean-Claude protested.

"I'll bet your goddam mother isn't even dead," snarled Jessica, wanting to hurt him. To make him go away. To rescind his very existence.

Paula rushed toward the boy and began to pummel him. He did not raise a hand to defend himself from her blows. For he was beginning to feel that he was, in some inexplicable way, guilty of a crime.

"Paula, stop hitting him this instant!"

Sheila rushed to pull the two children apart. Jean-Claude was crying softly. As soon as they were disengaged, he glanced fearfully at everyone and retreated, first tentatively, then more swiftly, up the stairs.

In a moment they heard the sound of his bedroom door closing.

Sheila looked at her traumatized daughters. This was all Bob's fault. They were innocent victims whose lives had just been permanently disfigured by the shrapnel of his infidelity.

And I was wrong too, she thought with anguish. I made the wrong decision. Now I see that I was only thinking of myself.

Just then a car pulled up outside. It was Bernie, dropping Bob off from their tennis match. Sheila watched her husband leap out, wave to his friend and start toward the house.

"It's Daddy," Sheila said. As if they hadn't sensed it from her face.

"I'll never speak to him again!" cried Jessica, who turned and started quickly for the stairs.

"Me either," Paula added, following her sister, leaving Sheila all alone.

She sighed as she watched her husband stride closer and closer.

She heard the door swing open.

"Sheila honey?"

"I'm in here, Robert," she said quietly. And knew she sounded like a stranger.

20

THEY SAT FACING ONE ANOTHER.

"How did she find out?" Bob asked.

"I don't know. Did you tell Bernie?"

He lowered his head. "Yeah."

"Well, Davey must have overheard the two of them talking. . . ."

"What're we gonna do?" he asked Sheila.

"Not *we*," she said firmly. "This is *your* problem."

"What do you expect me to do?" he said, unwilling to understand what she was making crystal clear.

"Send him home, Robert," she said curtly. "Now. Today."

She was right.

"Otherwise I'll take the girls and go," Sheila added. Not as a threat but as a simple statement of the alternative.

"Okay," he said, not putting up a struggle. Still, he waited for her to say something vaguely reassuring. Something that could help him face this harsh decision. But she said nothing more.

He rose, went numbly to the phone and dialed.

"They have one seat on tonight's flight," he reported, putting his hand over the receiver, "but it leaves at seven. . . ."

"You can make it if you hurry," she said quietly, not turning toward him.

"Okay," she heard him tell the airline. "The name is Beckwith—uh—I mean Guérin. Yes, we'll get there an hour before." He hung up and walked over to Sheila.

"I guess I'll have to tell him, huh?"

She looked up, but said nothing.

"Yeah," he murmured, answering himself. "I'll go up and help him pack."

She still did not respond. He turned, started out of the room, and up the stairs.

He was too preoccupied with what he had to say to notice that the phone was ringing.

"Hello, Sheila?"

"Yes."

"Gavin Wilson here. Have I—um—caught you at an awkward time?"

"Well, actually, I just got in and—uh—could I call you back? Are you in Washington?"

"No, that's just the point. I'll be brief. I can tell you're busy. I was thinking that I might just postpone Washington, if you were free—that is, willing to keep forging ahead with the revisions. I mean, I'd come down to you, of course."

"Gavin, I can't," she said.

"Sheila," he persisted, "you sound upset. Is everything all right?"

"Gavin, I'm sorry. Things are too confused. I can't talk now."

She hung up. And for a split second almost laughed. This can't be happening, she thought.

* * *

Bob knocked.

"Jean-Claude, may I come in?"

"Yes," he answered softly. Bob slowly opened the door. The little boy was curled up on his bed. He cast a shy and furtive glance at Bob.

"Can we talk?" asked Bob.

"Yes."

He was nervous, wondering what the boy was thinking.

"Uh—okay if I sit down?"

Jean-Claude nodded. And again glanced fleetingly at Bob.

He chose the chair farthest from the bed.

"I can't tell you how sorry I am about the . . . fight with Jessie and Paula. It was just something Davey Ackerman said to make trouble."

He paused.

"Jessie really wouldn't want to hurt you. You know that, don't you, Jean-Claude?"

Without looking up, the boy nodded. Slightly.

"I'm sorry about all this," Bob continued.

The boy looked up at him.

"Would you like me to go home?" he asked.

Bob was embarrassed by the child's perceptiveness.

"Uh—well, Jean-Claude, I think—we think it might be best for you."

He paused again. Then the boy said:

"When will I be leaving?"

Oh, Christ, thought Bob, he's being so damn good about this.

"Well, that depends," Bob answered, being deliberately vague to keep a rein on his own emotions, "but why don't I help you pack, just so we'll be ready?"

"That's all right," Jean-Claude answered. "I have only a few things."

"I'll help you," Bob insisted.

"No. There is no need. Do you want me to be ready now?"

Bob hesitated.

"Yes," he said at last. "That would make it easier. I mean . . . I'll be back in a while, okay?"

He got up, crossed the room, touched the boy's shoulder and went out.

He stood for a moment outside Jessica's door, gathering his courage. Then he knocked.

"Who is it?" Jessie snapped belligerently.

"Me. Your father. I want to talk to you."

"I have no father. Go away."

"Please, Jess, open up. Is Paula there?"

"No," Paula's voice retorted through the door. "I hate you more than *anything*."

"Jess?" Bob again tried appealing to his eldest. "I love you—"

"Go away and die," she said.

"Go away!" Paula shouted. "Leave Mom and us *alone!*"

Heartsick, Bob surrendered and began to walk away. Down the stairs, back to the living room.

Sheila was curled up in the easy chair, hugging her knees.

"He'll be ready in a little while," Bob said softly.

She did not reply.

"He's packing by himself. He didn't want my help."

Sheila still did not reply. But she had a selfish thought: I won't ever have to see that picture in the silver frame again.

"The girls won't talk to me," he added. "Shit. I've devastated them, haven't I? I mean, what the hell can they believe in now? They'll never get over this."

Sheila sat there, silent and unmoving.

He now realized this was going to remain a monologue. So he asked his wife a favor. Directly.

"Can you try and speak to them while I'm gone?"

She looked at him and asked simply, "What could I say?"

21

Instead of taking Route 6 all the way across the Cape, Bob turned off onto 6A at Orleans. Slower, but prettier. The "Cranberry Highway," with a view of the sea.

The boy had been stoically silent during the last hours before departure. He had packed and then dutifully waited in his room for Bob to come and get him. Bob had carried the green valise, Jean-Claude his flight bag. They walked down the stairs to the kitchen, where Sheila had prepared cheese sandwiches and coffee to fortify them for the journey to the airport.

While the girls remained hermetically sealed in Jessie's room, Sheila had pulled herself together. It could not now get worse. There was even a part of the summer left to try to make things better. Tomorrow would be the first day of the rest of their lives. When words fail, comfortable clichés are always nice to fall back on. She watched the man and the boy eat their sandwiches, and spoke the commonplaces the occasion called for.

"It was nice having you, Jean-Claude."

His mouth was full. He swallowed and politely answered, "Thank you, madame."

Bob was silent, exiled with his conflicts.

"I'm sure Jessie and Paula are sorry for that . . . misunderstanding."

Everyone knew they were still upstairs. For the preceding hours had been punctuated with their plangent imprecations. The house was wood, after all.

"Please say goodbye for me," said Jean-Claude.

"Of course."

When they were about to leave, Jean-Claude extended his hand. Sheila took it, and then leaned down to kiss him on the cheek.

As Bob watched her, he had his first coherent thought of the afternoon: Am I going to be doing that at the airport, in just three more hours?

They had been riding for barely thirty minutes. Bob tried to make conversation.

"You know, when we passed Orleans, back there, I forgot to tell you something."

He glanced at the boy sitting next to him, clutching his flight bag in his lap.

"It's a curious fact"—Bob rambled like an awkward tour guide—"but that's where they built the very first cable station for telegrams to France. There weren't any phones in those days. . . ."

"Oh," said the boy quietly.

What am I babbling about? Bob wondered. Cables? Yes, he then realized, it wasn't all that irrelevant. You were trying to tell him somehow that you'd still keep in touch. That there was a history of direct communication between Cape Cod and France. Did he understand?

What was he thinking?

They passed Sandwich and he did not comment on the funny name.

They crossed the Cape Cod Canal and did not speak.

"We'll miss you, Jean-Claude," said Bob.

Coward, don't you even have the guts to use the singular?

Speak for yourself, Bob. And they were just passing Plymouth.

"I've grown really fond of you," he added. There, I've done it. I've expressed my own feelings. Some of them anyway.

For a long while, the boy did not reply. At last, when they were scarcely an hour from Logan Airport, he spoke.

"Is it true, Bob?"

"What?"

"Are you really my father?"

Bob looked at him. He has a right to the truth, dammit.

"Yes, Jean-Claude, I am your father."

All right, curse me out, kid, I deserve it. For not telling you the minute I first met you, to assuage your grief. For not even telling you today, until you made me.

And now, knowingly this time, abandoning you once again.

"That makes me happy," said the little boy. Yet there was a tinge of sadness in his voice.

Bob glanced at him with an expression that asked: Why?

"My mother used to talk about my father. That he was kind and good. And funny. And . . ."

"Yes?"

"And when I met you, even when I saw you for the first time at the airport, I hoped that maybe my father might be someone like you."

This was my worst fear, thought Bob. Or was it

my best hope? That I would meet my son and he would like me—no, love me, imperfect as I am.

He reached over and touched the little boy. Jean-Claude took Bob's hand with both of his and held it tightly. Very tightly.

Bob could not look at him. He stared straight ahead, lying to himself that it was because he had to be a careful driver.

The boy still tightly held his hand.

And Bob said to himself: I can't let him go back. *I can't let go.*

22

CHILDHOOD HAD ABRUPTLY ENDED FOR JESSICA AND Paula.

As she stood at the top of the stairway, Sheila could hear them talking to one another.

"He's never gonna come back to this house," Paula insisted. "Never, never, never."

Jessie's tone of voice sounded strangely less agitated. "That's really up to Mom," she said.

There was a pause while Paula considered this.

"How could she even talk to him after what he's done?" she asked.

"I don't know," Jessie answered. "I just hope they don't really—you know—split. I mean, kids from broken homes are always screwed up."

Another silence while Paula tried to ponder the grown-up realities.

"Oh, Jessie, I'm so scared. Everything's different."

"Don't worry. I'll take care of you."

Yet another pause.

"But who'll take care of Mom?"

Sheila knocked, and opened the door. She found Jessie with her arms around Paula. They both looked relieved to see her. She sat down on the bed.

"Well, it's been quite a day, hasn't it?" And she made an effort to smile.

"What's gonna happen, Mom?" asked Paula anxiously.

"Well, Daddy will be back soon," she replied, "and we'll start to pick up the pieces."

"Are we ever gonna be happy again?" Paula asked. Nothing in her world seemed sure now.

"Of course we will. Look, the most painful part of growing up is discovering that nobody's perfect. Not even your parents."

"You are," said Paula.

"Nobody is," Sheila insisted.

Jessie looked at her mother's eyes. "You still love Daddy, don't you?"

Sheila nodded. "Jess, we've been happy for nearly twenty years. Happier than almost anyone." She hesitated and then let slip, "Almost perfect."

"God, Mom," Jessie said painfully. "Life's crappy."

Sheila weighed this judgment for a moment.

"Yes, darling," she acknowledged. "Sometimes it is."

Just then the doorbell rang. Could it be Bob already? The girls were certainly not prepared to face him. She wasn't even sure she was.

"I'll get it," she said.

He's trying to be considerate, she thought as she started downstairs. Instead of just barging in, he rang to warn us.

Sheila opened the door.

It was Gavin Wilson. She was speechless.

"Forgive me for intruding, Sheila," he said, looking ill at ease, "but you sounded a bit strange on the phone. I was rather concerned. Are you quite certain everything is all right?"

"Oh, yes. It's just that when you called, the children were . . ." She groped for a plausible excuse.

"Yes. Quite," he said, agreeing with her incompleted thoughts.

They were both a trifle awkward, standing there on the porch, not knowing quite what to say next.

"Aren't you supposed to be in Washington?" she asked, thinking, God, I must look a mess.

"It can do without me for another day, I think." Oh.

"Would you—uh—like to come in?" she asked. But Gavin sensed that she really did not want him to.

"Well, I'm afraid I've been presumptuous in rushing down. But I'm glad everything's all right. Look, I'm staying at the Inn. If I can—you know —be of help in any way, just ring. On the other hand, don't feel obliged to."

Shut up, Gavin, you're burbling again.

"That's very kind of you," said Sheila. And then added vaguely, "My husband ought to be back soon. He had to go to the airport."

"Oh?" said Gavin. "Some sort of emergency?"

"You might say so."

"Oh," said Gavin again.

To which Sheila replied, "I'm very touched by your thoughtfulness."

"Yes. Well. Uh—you know where to reach me, then," he answered shyly. He then turned and started back toward his rented car.

"Gavin," Sheila called. He stopped about ten yards from the porch.

"Yes?"

"Would you like to join us for a drink this evening—say, nine-thirty or so?"

"That would be splendid. Should I call and check first?"

"No, no. Just come by. Bob will be glad to meet you."

"Fine. Well, till then." He waved in a kind of half salute, turned and walked to his car.

How nice he is, thought Sheila. Going to all this trouble. Just for me.

Sheila and the girls were having dinner when the phone rang.

"Sheila?"

"Bob—is everything okay?"

"Uh—yes and no. We ran into an incredible traffic jam. We're still not at Logan and the flight's already taken off."

"Oh."

"Listen," he said, "there's only one sensible solution. We should stay over in Lexington so he can take the flight tomorrow. Don't you agree?"

She hesitated and then said:

"I suppose it makes sense."

"How are the girls?"

"A bit calmer."

"I'd like to say something to them. Will they talk to me?"

"I doubt it."

Just then a nasal voice intruded on the line.

"Deposit another forty cents for the next three minutes."

"Okay. Listen, Sheil," Bob said hastily. "I'll call you again when I get to the house."

"All right."

"I love you," he said quickly, just as the phone went dead. He hoped she had heard him. Because he had done a lot of rehearsing before making the call.

He put the receiver on the hook and started back

into the dining area of the Wellesley Howard John-
son's on Route 128.

Jean-Claude was sitting in a corner booth, picking
at his fried clams (it was eat-all-you-want fish
night). Bob sat down across from him.

"How would you like to stay another day?" he
asked. "We could sleep over at our house in Lexington. What do you think?"

"Oh, yes," said the boy.

23

FOR ONCE THE GIRLS NEEDED NO CAJOLING TO GET them to bed. They had earlier accepted the news of Bob's absence with apparent equanimity. Or at least emotional exhaustion.

But Sheila could not keep herself from feeling resentful. Even when he had called the airline, Bob seemed to be looking for excuses to stall. Maybe he had deliberately missed the flight. To steal another day with his son.

She was also angry because he had left her alone to deal with the girls, taking for granted, as usual, that she would handle it. He didn't even sound apologetic about staying away for the night. Don't we matter anymore? Where the hell are his priorities?

Gavin Wilson arrived at the stroke of nine-thirty. For some reason he looked slightly different. And then she realized: he was wearing a tie and jacket.

"Hello, Sheila." The tone of his voice matched the formality of his dress.

"Come in," she said. "Can I get you something to drink?"

"Please. Scotch and water, if that's convenient." He followed her inside.

"Ice?"

"Yes, please. I've been thoroughly Americanized."

When they entered the living room, he glanced around uneasily.

"Uh—Bob had to stay in Boston," Sheila said, and tried to sound as casual as possible.

"Oh? Any problem?"

"No. Of course not. Just a last-minute delay."

"Oh."

"Please sit down, Gavin. I'll get the drinks."

It came upon her unawares as she was opening the fridge. Suddenly the strain of all the pretense was too much for her. She closed the door, leaned on it and began to cry. Softly, steadily.

It was a relief. Now she realized just how much she'd wanted to break down. And for how long.

Suddenly she felt someone's arms around her.

Gavin had come into the kitchen without her even hearing him.

As he continued to hold her, he whispered, "Now, Sheila, are you or are you not going to tell me what the matter is?"

She could not move, trapped by the crosswinds of emotion.

"I don't know you," she said without turning.

"If it will make it any easier," he answered gently, "I've been checked for security by the FBI. That means I can be trusted with the most vital secrets."

She gave a little laugh. He was still holding her. She neither turned nor tried to move away. His voice now trembled slightly as he said:

"Anyway, for what it's worth, I think I'm falling in love with you."

She did not reply.

"Please answer me, Sheila. I had to work up a lot of courage to say that."

"Don't be silly, Gavin," she replied. He was still holding her.

"I know you've got every reason not to believe me. We've just met. And then of course I made that ridiculously clumsy pass in the restaurant. You don't know how sorry I am. I was so furious afterwards that I walked for nearly two hours along the Charles. I must really have looked miserable—even the muggers avoided me."

Is this man trying to say he really cares for me?

"I mean, dammit, it was awful of me not to realize that something was troubling you."

"It's all right," she said. It was merely an affirmative statement of her feelings, not a precise reply to his remarks.

"Listen," he continued, "I came here not just to apologize but to try and comfort you. Do you feel a little better now?"

"Yes."

"Good. Now then, go back to the sitting room and I'll fix us both that drink. Then maybe we can talk about what's bothering you. You having Scotch as well?"

She nodded yes.

"Then off you go."

He handed her a glass and sat down in the chair opposite her.

"Well?" he said.

"Well what?"

"You did understand what I was saying to you just now?"

She nodded.

"And?"

She looked down into her glass and then again at him.

"Gavin, I don't fool myself. You're—how can I

put it?—a kind of intellectual pinup. I, on the other hand—"

"Don't finish that sentence, Sheila. You are not only intelligent and beautiful, you're extremely sensitive, and, if my instinct is correct, like myself a member of FOBS."

"What's FOBS?"

"The Fellowship of Bruised Souls. Uh—I'm the founder, actually."

"You don't seem at all wounded to me."

"I've just learned to hide it better. A little cynicism goes a long way."

He paused. "I didn't really tell you the whole story the other night at dinner. When I left England and my wife didn't, it wasn't exactly Oxford she preferred as much as a certain Oxford don. A very nice professor of philosophy. So you see my being a 'pinup,' as you so flatteringly call it, can't really compensate for the fact that my own wife didn't think so."

Now his eyes betrayed the memory of unhappiness.

"Oh," said Sheila. "I'm sorry. I don't know what to say except that I think I know the feeling. How did you get over it?"

"I really haven't. I'm not quite sure I ever will completely. But time does help—regenerates one's capacity for hope. After a while you begin to believe you might actually meet someone you trust."

He looked at her.

"I really don't know where I am," she said. "I mean, so many things have happened to me all at once."

He took a breath and then asked gently, "Is there someone else in your husband's life, Sheila?"

She was dumbfounded.

"I understand," he said. "You can't talk about it. I'm sorry I brought it up."

But she had to say something.

"Gavin, things aren't quite the way they look. I mean—" She shook her head, unable to find words. "I mean I just couldn't explain it if I tried."

"Sheila, I withdraw my question—with apologies. It's really none of my bloody business."

She could not even say thank you.

"Some other time," he added, "when you feel you can. Or want to."

He stood up.

"Look. I know I should really go now. . . ."

She was about to protest, when he added:

"Really, it's the right thing for both of us."

She hesitated, and at last said, "Thank you, Gavin."

He took out his address book, tore a page from it and began scribbling.

"Now I'm giving you my home number in Washington and my White House extension. And I'm warning you—if I don't hear from you by the end of the week, I'll call you. I have to know you're all right."

She thought, Should I ask him to stay?

"I'm going to plan on spending a week in Cambridge right after Labor Day. But in the meantime, promise me you'll call. Even to talk about the weather. I just want to hear your voice. Please. Promise."

"Yes."

"Mommy, I can't sleep."

It was Paula, standing there in her pajamas.

"Oh, honey, I'll be up in a second," Sheila responded. And then introduced the stranger. "Gavin, this is my daughter Paula. Paula, this is Dr. Wilson from Washington."

"The one who wrote the books who's not as conceited as you thought?" Paula asked.

"Yes." Sheila smiled. And Gavin laughed.

"Hello, Dr. Wilson," Paula said.

"How do you do," said Gavin.

"It's past my bedtime," she added, by way of elucidation.

"Then you must hurry back to bed."

"Dr. Wilson is right," Sheila added.

"Will you tuck me in, Mom?" asked Paula.

"Of course."

"Great. I'll be waiting. Night, Dr. Wilson." And she was off to prepare for Sheila's visit.

"She's a lovely little girl," said Gavin. "Now are you sure you'll be all right on your own?"

"Yes," she answered.

She went with him to the door. He stopped and looked down at her.

"I would like very much to kiss you, but this is not the time. Good night, Sheila. I hope you won't forget anything I've said." He gently touched her cheek.

And walked out into the night.

Sheila watched his car drive off and thought, I wonder what would have happened if he'd kissed me.

24

Bob awakened slowly to the sound of rain. At first glance it seemed like a winter day. And felt like it, as he closed the window. The outside thermometer actually read 58 degrees. Winter on the Fourth of July. A statistical impossibility—except in Boston.

He padded down the hallway and peered into Jessie's room, where he had put Jean-Claude to bed for the night. The boy was still sleeping peacefully. The events of the previous day had clearly worn him out. Oh, God, thought Bob as he stared at the tranquil face. What am I going to do?

When Jean-Claude woke, they shared some rolls and coffee. And since the energetic rain showed no signs of fatigue, Bob abandoned plans to tour the sights in Lexington and Concord. Instead he drove to Cambridge and parked in the MIT faculty lot.

"This is where I teach," said Bob, as they splashed toward the entrance of his building.

Their footsteps echoed as they marched down the corridor to Bob's door.

Bob unlocked the office. It smelled musty as they entered.

"Is this where you do your mathematics?" the

boy asked, gazing at the wall-to-ceiling shelves of books.

"Some of it," Bob smiled.

"May I sit at your desk?"

"Sure."

The boy plopped onto Bob's chair and began to swivel from side to side. "I am Professor Beckwith," he pronounced in a kind of soprano-baritone. "Would you like to ask me some statistics, sir?"

"Yes," replied Bob. "What are the chances of this damn rain stopping today, Professor?"

"Mmm," said Jean-Claude, pondering earnestly. "You'll have to see me tomorrow about that." And then he giggled, enjoying his own joke. And sitting in his father's leather chair.

Bob sat down opposite Jean-Claude, in the seat usually reserved for his student visitors, and smiled at the boy. He seemed minuscule behind that desk, today preternaturally neat. Bob had swept away the clutter before leaving in June. In fact, all that was left besides the telephone was a picture of Sheila and the girls.

"I like it here," said Jean-Claude. "You can see all the sailboats on the river. Look—there are even some out in the rain."

Bob was usually so wrapped up in work that he rarely glanced out of the window. But the boy was right. His view was wonderful.

It was almost 3 P.M.

"I have an idea," said Bob. "If you don't mind a little walk, we could visit the Museum of Science. I think you might like it."

"Okay."

Bob found an old semi-operative umbrella and together they went out to brave the elements. They crossed Memorial Drive and walked along the river to Science Park.

As Bob expected, the museum was packed because of the bad weather. Jean-Claude stood hypnotized by the gaze of Spooky the Owl, the avian host of the place. Bob bought him a Spooky T-shirt. Which he immediately put on.

"On *top* of your other clothes?"

"Yes."

"Why?"

"Why not?"

They then waited their turn so that Jean-Claude could explore the lunar surface and climb up into the Apollo landing module. He waved at Bob, who now stood several hundred thousand miles away.

"*Salut* from the moon."

Bob smiled. He offered Jean-Claude his hand to help him out of the spaceship, and after that the little boy did not let go. They went up to the second floor, bought ice cream cones and engaged the plexiglass Transparent Woman in conversation. Bob was impressed with how much anatomy the boy already knew.

"Do you want to be a doctor when you grow up?" he asked.

"Perhaps. Or maybe a professor."

A man's voice rudely dispelled their reverie.

"How're you making out?" he asked.

Bob turned. He was being addressed by a middle-aged man with a boy and a girl in tow.

"Isn't it a bitch, these custody days?" he continued. "At least if it wasn't raining I could take 'em to a parade or the ball game. I bet they're as sick of this museum as I am."

Bob did nothing to encourage dialogue, but his very silence seemed to inspire the bore.

"My ex took 'em here last week, can you believe it? I thought she'd already ripped off everything I had. Now she's after my last option to entertain the kids. By the way, my name's Phil Harlan. Interested in joining forces?"

Bob looked at Harlan. And Harlan's kids. They seemed as miserable as their father. And then he thought of his daughters. We could never come to this, he told himself. Harlan and his lifestyle made him shudder.

"Sorry, we've got other plans," he answered coolly, and started to walk off with Jean-Claude.

"Well, catch you some Saturday in the fall, huh?" Harlan was undaunted.

"Maybe," Bob muttered without turning.

In the museum souvenir shop, Jean-Claude asked Bob to buy him a postcard of the lunar surface. To send to his friend Maurice in Montpellier. He dictated the message, which Bob dutifully transcribed:

> *Tu vois, Maurice, moi aussi je peux voler!*
> *Ton ami,*
> *Jean-Claude*

The message puzzled Bob.

"What do you mean, you can fly too?"

"Maurice says he built a spaceship in his cellar. He was going to fly to Sète to visit me, but his mother found out, so he couldn't come."

"Oh," said Bob, biting his lip to keep from smiling.

"But he made me promise not to tell anyone."

"I won't," said Bob, feeling happy to be trusted.

He bought a newspaper. Not to check on flights, for he knew they left each evening at seven, but to find something to do.

"Hey," he said, "there's supposed to be a great

outdoor concert tonight, just across the river. I wonder if they've canceled it."

The friendly lady at the souvenir desk overheard and answered, "Not *this* concert, sir. It's Mr. Fiedler's golden anniversary with the Pops."

"Thanks, ma'am," said Bob, and then turned to Jean-Claude. "We might get a little wet, but it could be fun."

"Is it jazz?"

"No. Does it matter?"

"No," said the boy.

25

THEY WALKED BACK ALONG THE RIVER TO BOB'S car and he took out the ancient blanket he always kept in the trunk. Then after a detour to buy submarine sandwiches, they crossed the Harvard Bridge and strolled to the Esplanade, the crescent of green grass which embraced Hatch Shell, the hemispheric shelter for musicians in the rain.

Several thousand diehard fans were camped in defiance of the elements, having improvised tents, tepees, lean-tos and the like. Bob and Jean-Claude spread their blankets as close as possible to the shell.

"If we're gonna have wet bottoms, let's at least get a good view," Bob said, and offered Jean-Claude an enormous sandwich.

"Must I?" asked the boy. "My stomach hurts a little."

"Don't worry," Bob assured him, thinking it was probably nerves. "Eat what you can."

"Okay," he sighed, and began pecking away desultorily.

About an hour later, a storm of applause drowned out the drizzle. The venerable conductor was striding to the podium. The crowd rose to its feet and shouted, "We love you, Arthur."

Bob explained. "The man with all the white hair is a big celebrity. He's even more important than the music."

"He looks like *Père Noël*," said the boy.

"You're right," Bob answered, "but he doesn't just look like Father Christmas. He looks like *everybody's* father. That's his appeal, I guess."

Then Bob had a curious thought. I've never really looked at Fiedler this close, but there's something about him that reminds me of Dad.

And he remembered the many happy excursions he had taken with his own father. The Phillies games. Saturday matinees with Ormandy and the Philadelphia Orchestra. Camping in the Poconos. Just the two of them. Suddenly he missed his father terribly.

Fiedler raised his baton and the concert began. The opening number was "When Johnny Comes Marching Home."

During the next half hour the rains intensified.

"I think we should go," said Bob.

"Oh, no, please," said the boy.

"Okay," said Bob with some reluctance. He glanced at his watch. Eight-forty. The plane for Paris was already over the Atlantic.

The finale was the "1812 Overture," complete with pealing church bells and cannon shots from a little howitzer. Jean-Claude was ecstatic, especially when he recognized what melody the brasses were blaring against the swirl of strings.

"It's *La Marseillaise*," he shouted, leaping to his feet.

"Yes," said Bob. "It's a surprise for you."

As the music continued, the boy was transported. He was clapping even before it ended, and continued to applaud as the orchestra segued into "Stars and Stripes Forever." Now the whole waterlogged crowd rose to its feet, singing, shouting and marching in place. A glorious pandemonium.

Suddenly the sky exploded with lights—red, white, green, yellow, blue.

"*Regarde, Papa,*" cried the boy. "*Les feux d'artifice!*"

Bob picked him up and put him on his shoulder, so he could have a better view of the dazzling fireworks. As he did, he could not help noticing that although the air was cold, the boy seemed strangely warm. Too warm.

"Come on, Jean-Claude, let's go back to the car."

Still carrying the boy, Bob began to walk toward the bridge. Jean-Claude's gaze remained transfixed by the multicolored bombs bursting in air.

By the time they reached the MIT parking lot, Jean-Claude was shivering. Bob put his hand to the boy's forehead. It was very hot.

"Let's go up to my office and change you into some dry clothes," he said.

"Okay," said the boy, sounding very subdued.

Bob opened the trunk, grabbed the green valise, and the two of them hurried toward the entrance to his office.

Upstairs, he dried Jean-Claude with paper towels from the men's room. The boy seemed suddenly so small and frail, all bony shoulders and skinny legs. But every limb was blazing.

"Would you like me to get you some tea from the machine?" Bob asked.

"No, I don't want anything," replied Jean-Claude.

Damn, thought Bob, I've given him cramps from junk food and now I've frozen him into a fever. Great father.

And then he realized. I can't take him back to Lexington. I don't know how to handle a sick child. He put his windbreaker around the boy and, before he lost the nerve, dialed Sheila at the Cape.

"Bob, where are you? It's raining like hell here."

"Here too," he replied, "and the fog is terrible. I couldn't let him fly in this weather."

"Oh," she said blandly. And then added, "I suppose that's wise."

There was a silence.

"Listen, Sheil, he's been soaked and I think he's got a fever. Maybe I could take him to Mass General, but—"

"Is he that sick?"

"No. I mean, I'm not sure. Look—can I bring him back just for tonight?"

There was another pause.

"Bob, the girls are still very upset. Being cooped up all day hasn't helped matters." She sighed. "But I don't think it's good for you to stay away anymore. It's beginning to look like you've left."

Bob was enormously relieved.

"Yes. Anyway, it'll only be for a day or so. I mean, we can't let a sick child travel. Don't you agree?"

She hesitated. He waited nervously.

"I don't think you should stay away any longer," she repeated. Avoiding one issue, and speaking directly to the more important one: their marriage.

26

THE ROAD WAS SLICK AND DARK. BOB DROVE TOO fast. The boy was clearly getting sicker by the minute. He sat quietly, holding his stomach, now and then emitting a barely audible moan.

"Shall I play the radio?" Bob asked.

"Okay. . . ."

He put on WCRB, desperately hoping that the music would somehow soothe the child.

No one was on the highway. The storm seemed to have discouraged even the state police. He reached the Cape Cod Canal in record time. And he continued to push the car along Route 6.

The nearer he got, the angrier the heavens became.

He skidded as he turned onto Pilgrim Spring Road. Fortunately, he spun off into heavy mud and regained control almost immediately.

He glanced at the boy. Jean-Claude hadn't even noticed the near accident. He was oblivious to everything except his stomach pains.

Bob braked sharply as he pulled up in front of the house. Rain pelted the windshield. He breathed a deep sigh of relief. They had made it in one piece.

He looked over at the boy. His eyes were closed, his head leaning against the door.

"We're here, Jean-Claude," he whispered, stroking his hair. "It's gonna be all right now."

The boy did not react.

"Are you okay?" Bob asked.

The boy nodded.

"Do you feel well enough to walk—or should I carry you?"

"I can walk," he said slowly.

"Good. Then when I count to three, we each get out our own side and hurry into the house. Okay?"

"Okay."

Bob counted, and then stepped out into the downpour. He looked quickly across to the other side of the car, saw Jean-Claude's door open, and then rushed for the shelter of the porch.

Sheila was waiting alone in the living room. Though it had been just over twenty-four hours since they had seen one another, their awkwardness made it feel like years. She looked at her husband, soaked with rain and remorse.

"Are you okay?" she asked.

"Yeah. You?"

"Surviving," she answered.

"Where are the girls?"

"I sent them to their room. I didn't think this was the time for confrontations." She seemed to be glancing over his shoulder.

"Is something wrong?" he asked.

"Where's Jean-Claude?"

"He's—" Bob turned. The boy was not behind him. He was not anywhere. He turned back to Sheila. "Maybe he was too scared to come in."

"Let's get him," she said.

He rushed to the porch and saw nothing but the

ink-black storm. Then a bolt of lightning sliced the sky, briefly illuminating the driveway.

He was lying face down, a few steps from the car, the rain slapping his motionless body.

"Jesus!" Bob gasped. He ran to the boy and turned him over.

"He's unconscious," he shouted to Sheila, who was standing on the porch.

"Bring him in. I'll call a doctor!" she shouted back.

"No—it looks bad. I'm gonna take him right to the hospital."

In an instant she was by his side, looking at the child as the downpour drenched them both. She felt his forehead as Bob lifted him.

"He's absolutely boiling!" She opened the car door as Bob gently placed him inside. "I'll come with you."

"No. Go in and warn the hospital."

"Are you sure?"

"Go on, Sheila, please." He was almost hysterical. She nodded and ran back toward the house.

From a lighted window on the second floor, two pairs of eyes watched Bob's car splash down the driveway onto the road. Jessica and Paula wondered what new catastrophe had just entered their lives.

Bob drove to Hyannis like a man possessed. The boy was silent, his breathing short and rapid. And his forehead began to grow disturbingly cold. Now and then his delirium abated and he would utter a single word: *"Maman."*

The emergency room was a madhouse. The stormy holiday roads had yielded more than the statistical expectation of traffic accidents. But as Bob, holding Jean-Claude in his arms, announced himself, a young harried-looking intern rushed out.

"Bring him right into the examining room," he said.

Bob watched him check Jean-Claude's pulse and then immediately begin palpating the boy's abdomen. He heard the physician mutter, "Oh, shit," and thought to himself, That's a great diagnosis. This kid must be a student or something. I've got to get a real doctor. The young man snapped an order to a hovering nurse: "Get an IV into him immediately, and put in two g.m.'s of ampicillin and sixty m.g.'s of gentamicin. Prepare a nasogastric tube and have somebody get John Shelton fast."

She rushed off. The intern took the thermometer from Jean-Claude's mouth, squinted at it and again muttered to himself.

"What's wrong?" Bob asked impatiently.

"Can you step outside, sir?"

"I'll be right back," he told Jean-Claude, touching his icy cheeks. "Don't be afraid of anything." The boy nodded slightly. He looked terrified.

"Okay. What?" Bob demanded the instant they had left the room.

"Peritonitis," said the intern. "There's purulent fluid all over his peritoneal cavity."

"What the hell does that mean, dammit?"

"A burst appendix. His fever's 105 degrees. We've got to operate as soon as possible. We're sending for our best general surgeon. We think he's out on his boat—"

"Isn't there anybody here?" Bob asked, praying that there was someone already on the grounds more competent than this nervous kid.

"Dr. Keith is already in the OR with a patient. Really bad car accident. Besides, he's an orthopedic surgeon. Our best bet is to wait for Dr. Shelton."

"What do we do in the meanwhile?"

"He's very dehydrated, so I'm giving him intravenous fluid. And a large dose of antibiotics."

"And that's it?" Bob asked. "Can't we do anything else while we're waiting for this big shot?"

"We could be calm," said the intern pointedly. "Perhaps you might want to register him while you're waiting. . . ."

"Yeah," he said. "Okay. Thanks. Sorry." He turned away.

"Patient's name?" He told the registering clerk, spelling it for her slowly.

"Address?" He gave the Wellfleet house.

"Occupation?"

"Child," said Bob sarcastically, and then gave the boy's age.

"Religion?" He didn't know. The clerk looked displeased. "None," Bob said. She looked even more displeased. "Uh—I suppose Catholic." That answer, it seemed, was satisfactory.

Less so was the fact that there was no Blue Cross, Blue Shield or other medical plan. Bob's offer to pay was looked at askance.

"Mr. Beckwith," a voice called from down the corridor. "Good news!"

It was the intern, who ran up, breathless and sweating.

"What?" Bob asked.

"Dr. Shelton was home on account of the weather. He's just come in now."

"Great," Bob replied. And they both charged down the hall.

He had streaks of gray in his hair and looked, thank heavens, calm and experienced. His manner was in fact a bit too unemotional.

"Have we the permission to operate?" Shelton asked the intern.

"I haven't gotten around to it, sir."

Shelton turned to Bob.

"Where are the boy's parents?" he asked.

"They're . . . dead," Bob answered.

"Well, someone has to sign *in loco parentis*. Are you his guardian?"

"No. It's a man named Venarguès in France."

"Well, then he'll have to give us permission by telephone. That's legal if there's a second person listening."

No, thought Bob, there isn't time. I haven't even got Louis's number with me. It's somewhere in my desk.

"Uh—can't I sign?" Bob asked.

"You have no legal authority," said Shelton. "Why don't we get this Frenchman on the phone. The child is very sick."

"Then operate," Bob ordered. "Operate *now*."

"I can understand your concern, Mr. Beckwith. But surgeons, like everyone else, must live by the rules."

"Don't worry about a malpractice suit, dammit," Bob said angrily. "I'll indemnify you."

The surgeon remained phlegmatic and persistent. "Mr. Beckwith, my French is fluent. I can explain the entire situation to this Monsieur Venarguès."

Bob was desperate.

"Doctor, may I tell you something in confidence?"

"We've both taken the Hippocratic oath," said Shelton, nodding in the direction of the intern.

"May I speak to you alone?" said Bob, steeling himself.

"Uh—I'll check on Dr. Keith's progress," said the fidgety young man. "We'll be using OR two." And he dashed off. Bob and Shelton were alone.

"Yes?" said the surgeon.

"I can sign *in loco parentis*." Bob feared this uptight martinet might think it was a dodge.

"What precisely is your relationship?"

"I—I'm his father."

"But you just told me—"

"Out of wedlock," Bob said quickly. "His mother is Dr. Nicole Guérin. She's on the medical faculty at Montpellier, France. I mean, was. She died a month ago."

Bob's intuition was right. The irrelevant fact that the boy's mother had been a medical colleague made a curiously positive impression on Dr. Shelton.

"Is this really the truth?" he asked.

"Call my wife. She'll verify it," said Bob.

The doctor was convinced.

The operation dragged on and on. Bob sat on a plastic chair in the now empty waiting room and tried to control his feeling of frantic helplessness. It was impossible. He blamed himself for everything. At about a quarter to three he caught sight of the intern.

"Excuse me, Doctor," he called out meekly. "May I see you for a moment?" His attitude toward the young physician had changed markedly.

"Yes, Mr. Beckwith?"

"How serious is peritonitis?"

"Well, in young children it can be a pretty dicey thing."

"Meaning what? Can it be fatal?"

"Well, sometimes in children . . ."

"Jesus!"

"Dr. Shelton is really a fine surgeon, Mr. Beckwith."

"Still, there's a chance he could die, isn't there?"

"Yes, Mr. Beckwith," he said quietly.

"Hello, Sheila:"

"Bob—I've been so worried. Is he all right?"

"He's got a burst appendix. They're operating right now."

"Should I come over?"

"No. There's no point. Stay with the girls. I'll call as soon as there's news."

"Will he be all right?" she asked, hearing the panic in his voice.

"Yes, of course," he replied, trying to believe it, so he could at least convince her.

"Well, call me the instant you know. Please, honey. The girls are very upset too."

"Yeah. Try not to worry. Give them my love."

Bob hung up and walked back to his chair. He sat down and put his head in his hands. And at last gave in to the terrible sorrow he had, by some miracle, been able to suppress for the past six hours.

27

B<small>RILLIANT</small> <small>LECTURE</small>, B<small>OB</small>," <small>SAID</small> R<small>OBIN</small> T<small>AYLOR</small> of Oxford.

"*Comme d'habitude*," said René Moncourget of the Sorbonne.

"Especially considering the hardships of your journey," added Daniel Moulton, chief of IBM in Montpellier. "Just to make your way here during all the strikes was nothing short of heroic."

Indeed, for Robert Beckwith of MIT to reach southern France during the turbulent days of May 1968 had been a Herculean task. But the hardest labor was not so much having to fly to Barcelona, then rent an asthmatic car to drive across the Pyrennees all the way to Montpellier. It was that the entire expedition was in the company of his colleague P. Herbert Harrison.

For instead of marvcling at the beauty of the Mediterranean or the splendors of the Côte Vermeille, Harrison held forth incessantly on academic politics. Or more specifically, why he disliked everyone in the profession.

"*Except you, of course, Bob. You've always been decent to me. And naturally I've been true blue to you. Have I once complained that by seniority I*

*should be chairman? No, it's just our wretched col-
leagues—boring mediocrities. Whom, after all, did
the French invite to this congress? And do you
know what that snide fool Jamison said to me just
before we left?"*

*"Say, Herb, we're going to pass right by Nar-
bonne. Don't you think we could take a half hour
or so to look around? The cathedral is—"*

*"I think we'd better press on, Bob. I mean, we
do have a commitment and it's likely with this un-
godly French mess they haven't even gotten our
cable."*

*"Yeah. Well, would you mind taking the wheel
for a bit, Herb?"*

*"Equity bids no less, Bob. Still, you seem to be
enjoying yourself, so why stand on ceremony? Besides, you know what Mrs. Harrison says about my
driving."*

Oh, God, Bob thought, what did I ever do to
deserve this? Why the hell couldn't Sheila have
come? She seems to have a way of charming this
asshole into silence.

As if the drive had not been sufficiently grueling,
The Hôtel Métropole had placed the American professors Beckwith and Harrison in adjoining rooms.
Bob was therefore subjected to relentless carping
after each day's meetings. Everyone in the world of
statistics, it seemed, was second rate. No wonder
Harrison had insisted on giving the final lecture on
the final afternoon. Though he loathed his colleagues, he still dreaded their criticism. His fat head
was matched only by his thin skin.

After his own paper, Bob was too relieved and
euphoric even to care what Harrison might say
about *him*. And so he began to ease away from the
group of well-wishers.

"Aren't you coming to lunch with us, Bob?" called Harrison.

"Thanks, Herb. But I'd like to unwind a bit."

Harrison now sidled up to him.

"Beckwith, you can't leave me with Moncourget and those other characters. They're lightweights. I won't be sharp for my paper. I mean, that Taylor is an absolute—"

"Sorry, Herb, but I'm really too keyed up. If I can take a little walk I'll be fresher for your performance."

"No, Bob," the colleague pleaded. "Besides, it's dangerous. Didn't you hear about the bomb they threw?"

"That was last week, Herb."

"But there are bound to be reprisals. The concierge told me there'd be some big march today. Thousands of rabid students in the streets." (Harrison always cringed when he said "students.")

"That's okay," Bob replied. "I've had rabies shots." And he started down the cobblestone street.

"Beckwith, you're deserting a colleague," called Harrison.

Tough shit, thought Bob. And prayed for the day he might actually shout it.

He headed toward the Place de la Comédie, stopping every so often to admire the elegant eighteenth-century town houses. The closer he came to the center of town, the louder became the noise of the marching students. He could not help noticing police vans crouched in the tinier off-streets. Like tigers waiting to pounce. What could they possibly be expecting?

"*Salaud! Putain de flic! Espèce de fachaud!*"

Ahead of him in the narrow street, several policemen had stopped two female students in jeans.

They had made them turn and place their hands against the wall. What kind of bust was this? he wondered. The cops were frisking the girls, especially their hindquarters. They can't be carrying weapons, Bob thought. Their pants are too tight.

He drew closer. The dialogue between the police and the women was growing steadily more acrimonious, though Bob could not understand all they were saying. He stopped about ten feet away to watch the scene.

"Hé toi—qu'est-ce que tu fous là?"

One of the policemen had noticed Bob and politely asked him what the fuck he thought he was doing.

"Nothing," he replied in his best Yale French. But now both officers were moving toward him.

"Tes papiers," ordered the one who had just addressed him.

His papers? Both his passport and his driver's license were back at the hotel. And his tie and jacket were back in the lecture hall. He didn't look too professorial. The two policemen were now upon him. *"Et alors?"* said the junior officer.

"I'm an American," said Bob, hoping that would solve matters.

"Parle Français, conard," snarled the larger officer.

"I'm a professor," Bob said, again in French.

"Sure," said the cop, "and my ass is ice cream."

"Leave him alone," called one of the two girls, "or he'll have Nixon bomb your *préfecture!*"

This threat did not deter the officers, who were now crowding Bob against a wall. "Where the hell are your papers?" they demanded, grabbing him by the shirt.

"In my hotel, dammit," he said angrily. "Métropole, room 204."

"Bullshit," said the cop, and slammed him against the house. Bob was now frightened and put up his hand to fend off a blow he sensed imminent.

And he was right, for he suddenly felt a sharp crack at his forehead, which stunned him. One of the girls ran up and began a torrent of abuse which somehow made an impression on Bob's aggressors. They began to back off, warning, "Next time carry your papers."

Bob was shaking as they marched to their car and, ignoring the women, sped off.

"Thanks," he said to the girl who had saved him. She was slender and raven-haired. "What exactly did you tell him?"

"I just showed the pig you were wearing your hello card."

"My what?"

She pointed to his shirt pocket. Pinned to it was his conference name tag, courtesy IBM:

HELLO! MY NAME IS:
Robert Beckwith
MIT
U.S.A.

"Sorry about your head," said the girl. "You'd better let me take a look at it."

Bob put his hand to his temple. It was swollen and bleeding. And starting to throb.

"The bastard punched me," he muttered. He had never been struck in his life. "Maybe I should go to the hospital."

"No need. I'll make a house call. Or you might say a street call."

"You're a doctor?"

"Yes. And Simone over there is a third-year student. Come on, I've got my stuff in the trunk."

Bob walked, a bit unsteadily, to the red Dauphine convertible the girls were driving. Simone opened the trunk and handed the doctor her kit. She opened a bottle and began to dab Bob's wound.

"It's fairly superficial," she said as she placed several gauze sponges on the injured area and wrapped a pressure dressing around his forehead.

"How's your equilibrium?"

"I don't know."

"I'd better take a closer look," she replied. "That wasn't a fist he hit you with—it was his *matraque*."

"His billy club? Jesus! What did I do?"

"Watch him feel us up without a ticket." She smiled. "Come into the café down there. Can you walk okay?"

"Yes."

Once inside, she led him to a fairly dark corner, took out an ophthalmoscope and began to peer into Bob's eyes, her forehead close to his.

"What are you doing?" he asked.

"Smelling your aftershave lotion," she replied. "It's sexy."

Bob gave a nervous laugh. They were standing head to head.

"No, seriously," he asked again.

"I'm checking your pupillary reflexes."

"I'm not a pupil, I'm a teacher," he joked.

"You're not a comedian, either," she replied.

"Am I okay?" he asked seriously.

"I'm pretty sure, but the light in here isn't terribly good. I suggest you go back to your hotel and lie down with a cold compress. And take two aspirins."

"Ah, aspirin—now I know you're a serious doctor."

The blue-jeaned physician threw back her dark hair and laughed.

"Do you want a ride?" she asked, still smiling.

"No, thanks. I think a walk would do me good." He started out of the café. She called after him.

"Listen, if you don't feel better, be sure to come to the hospital before six."

"Why six?"

"Because that's when I get off. Ask for Dr. Guérin. Nicole Guérin."

28

Beckwith, are you in there?"

Someone was pounding on Bob's head—or was it the door of his hotel room? Gradually he realized it was the latter. He stood up and started slowly towards the noisy door, and opened it.

"You missed my lecture, Beckwith." It was Harrison.

"Sorry, Herb. I ran into a little trouble."

He finally noticed Bob's bandage. "What happened to your head?"

"Two cops . . ."

"Oh. Have you seen a doctor?"

"Yeah. In the street."

"Bob, you're not making any sense. We'd better get out of here. This country's in chaos and the streets are full of wretched students."

"Thanks for dropping by," said Bob woozily. "I've got to lie down now."

"Beckwith, you forget I'm delivering my paper again in Salzburg day after tomorrow. We've got to start driving immediately."

"Herbert, I've just been mugged. I'm in no shape to drive anywhere."

P. Herbert remained single-minded. "Bob, if we

drive to Milan you could get a plane to Boston, and I could fly on to Salzburg. Come on. The hotel could be bombed at any moment."

"Relax, Herb. Don't be paranoid. We'll get a good night's sleep and leave first thing in the morning."

"Impossible. Absolutely out of the question. I have a professional duty to discharge and I won't jeopardize my good name."

"Then you'll have to drive your*self*, Herb." (That'll call your bluff.)

"Very well," said the colleague heroically. "Where are the keys?"

Though a bit surprised, Bob was still willing to part with the car if it meant getting rid of Harrison. He reached into his pocket and handed over the keys.

"I feel bad leaving you like this," said P. Herbert, not looking at all remorseful. "How will you get out?"

"When the strike ends, I'll fly through Paris."

"But how will you contact Sheila? They don't seem to be taking any calls. Not even overseas."

"Well, you might be kind enough to phone her from Austria, okay? Don't mention my head. Just say the IBM guys asked me to stay a few more days and I'll call her as soon as the phones work."

"I'll be glad to."

"Thanks."

"That's all right. And you can reimburse me when I see you in Cambridge."

Bob eyed this obnoxious pinhead and thought, I'll reimburse you with my foot. But he couldn't actually say it, since he needed this guy to call Sheila.

"Thanks, Herb. Just make sure she knows I'm safe."

"See you around the campus, then."

"Yeah. Bon voyage."

As Bob closed the door, he screamed inwardly, I hope you drive off a goddam cliff, you selfish bastard. And then he slumped back onto the bed and fell asleep again.

He awoke to the tolling of bells. Five o'clock. His head was throbbing. He decided he ought to go to the hospital, after all.

The taxi rattled down Boulevard Henri Quatre and let him off just outside the emergency entrance of the Hôpital Général. Inside it was extremely crowded. Bob's name was taken and he was told to sit and wait. Which he did. On a hard wooden bench. After forty minutes he began to run out of patience. Maybe he should ask for that young doctor. What was her name—Guérin?

"We do have a Dr. Guérin," said the nurse in charge. "But she is in Pathology. Monsieur will kindly be seated and await the appropriate physician."

"Could you page her anyway? Say it's for Professor Beckwith."

She reluctantly complied. Within minutes Nicole Guérin breezed into the emergency room, clad in a white coat, her dark hair tied back in a ponytail.

"Follow me," she said to Bob, and led him briskly down a corridor. She stopped by a door marked RADIOLOGIE.

"Please step in here," she said.

The room was crammed with x-ray paraphernalia. A white-haired technician appeared to be in the process of closing shop. Nicole addressed him.

"Paul, I need cranial x-rays on the patient—to check for possible fracture."

"Now? But Nicole I am just going off for dinner—"

"Now, Paul. If you please."

"Very well," he sighed. "I capitulate to your smile."

Some fifteen minutes later, she was studying the inside of Bob's skull.

"Are my brains intact?" he quipped, to cover his anxiety.

"I'm not a psychiatrist," she smiled. "But I don't see any signs of fracture. You might have a mild concussion, but there's no way of determining that from these photographs. Basically, I think you're just 'shook up,' as you say in America."

"What should I do?" he asked.

"For the moment sit down and I'll re-dress your wound."

As she wrapped a new bandage around his head, Bob made polite conversation.

"I guess you don't do this sort of thing too often. I mean, being a pathologist."

"I'm only a specialist two days a week," she replied. "The rest of the time I'm a real doctor. You know, broken arms, measles, crying babies. In Sète, where I live. Do you know Sète?"

"Doctor, all I've seen is the inside of a lecture room and the chamber of commerce tour. You know —Roman ruins, Le Peyrou, the aqueduct . . ."

"Fascinating," she said sarcastically. "And you'll return to MIT without seeing the lovely fishing village where the poet Valéry was born and died? I can't allow that. Look, I'm off duty—let me take you right now. It's the perfect time of day."

"Uh—I don't think I could," said Bob.

"A previous engagement?"

"Well, sort of . . ." (I'm not only engaged, I'm married.)

Her dark brown eyes fixed on him. She spoke good-humoredly.

"Be frank—if I were a middle-aged man you would have accepted, right?"

He was embarrassed.

"Come on, Professor, the sea air will do you good. And, if you like, that's a medical order."

Before he knew it, they were in her red Dauphine, speeding south on the N 108. And she was right. The breeze coming off the ocean did clear his head considerably. And his mood.

"Where'd you learn such fluent English, Doctor?"

"Nicole," she corrected him. "We are in the midst of the new French Revolution, so everyone is on a first-name basis. Anyway, I spent a year in your city."

"Cambridge?"

"Well, Boston, actually. I had a clerkship in pathology at the Mass General. It was absolutely wonderful."

"Why didn't you stay on?"

"Oh, I was tempted. And my department head was willing to pull the necessary strings. But in the end I decided that even the greatest medical facilities couldn't compensate for what I have in Sète."

"Which is?"

"Well, the sea. And a very special feeling of being home."

"You mean family?"

"No. They're all gone. The villagers are my family. But I was born here and I want to die here. Besides, they could use a young doctor. Also my clinic is right above the best bakery in France."

"What about Montpellier?"

"I just keep the affiliation in case I need to hospitalize my Sétois."

"You seem very happy," said Bob.

She looked at him with a smile. Her bronzed face glowed in the setting sun.

"Oh, some people think I'm crazy. I actually turned down a post in Paris. But since I live by my own definitions, I can say I'm a very happy woman. Are you happy, Bob?"

"Yes," he replied, and seizing the opportunity, added, "I'm very happily married."

They flew along the highway, the Mediterranean on their left.

29

SÈTE WAS LIKE A LITTLE VENICE. EXCEPT FOR THREE small bridges, the old port was completely encircled by canals.

The restaurant reverberated with loud conversations in southern dialect, raucous laughter and song, and the obbligato of clinking glasses.

"What are they celebrating?" Bob asked as they sat at an outdoor table.

"Oh, the day's catch, the revolution—or maybe just life," she replied.

She ordered a *bourride*, the local fish stew, and a white wine from Narbonne. Bob grew increasingly uneasy. This was getting more and more like a date. Maybe he should have left with Harrison, after all.

"Are you married?" he asked.

"No. And I never will be," she replied softly.

"Oh," he said.

She reached across the table and touched his hand. "But I don't steal husbands, Bob. I'm not a Circe. I have been involved with married men, but only by mutual consent."

Somehow her hand did not have the reassuring effect it was ostensibly supposed to.

"Nicole! *Salut, ma vielle, ma jolie professeur de*

médecine!" A voice more like the growl of a bear heralded the arrival of a red-faced old man wearing an open shirt.

"Ah," Nicole whispered to Bob. "We're about to be honored by a visit from the mayor himself."

"*Et comment va ma petite génie, ma jolie doctoresse?*"

The old man threw his arms around Nicole and they kissed each other on both cheeks. He then turned to Bob.

"*Salut. Je m'apelle Louis. Et toi?*"

"This is Bob," said Nicole, "a professor from America."

"America?" said Louis, an eyebrow raised. "Are you for or against the war?"

"Against," said Bob.

"Good," said the mayor, sitting down uninvited. "This calls for a drink." And he signaled the owner to bring out some of his usual *muscat*. He then lit a cigarette and turned back to Nicole's guest.

"So, Bobbie, what do you think of our revolution, eh?"

"Well, I really haven't seen much more than the end of a cop's club."

"They struck him?" Louis asked Nicole.

She nodded. "It was early in the morning and they needed to warm up."

"*Salauds,*" muttered Louis. "They should have been out looking for the bastards who bombed the GCT."

"What's that?" Bob asked Nicole. He vaguely recalled Harrison's mentioning a bombing.

"Our big labor union," she replied. "A few days ago somebody tossed a Molotov cocktail at their office."

"*Fachauds,*" Louis growled on. "But I tell you, Bobbie, the workers are going to win this one.

They've got the government pissing in their pants. I say the Grenelle accord will be just one step in the inevitable process. By the way, what do you think of Pompidou?"

"I think he's got every right to be nervous," Bob replied.

Louis laughed heartily. "Nervous? He hasn't got a dry pair of pants. For once the workers have made those big shots in Paris wake up. You know, we're not some sleepy fishing village. We have industry all around. They're building refineries in Frontignan. And we also manufacture *engrais*."

"What's *engrais?*" Bob asked Nicole.

"Fertilizer," she replied.

"Nicole," said Louis, "did I tell you the fantastic slogan I conceived for the *engrais* workers? Listen. 'No money, no shit!' Fantastic, eh?" And he roared with self-appreciation.

"That's—uh—original," said Bob.

"Listen," said Louis, precipitously switching the subject. "I have to go off and meet some of my *enragés*. You two come by tomorrow for lunch with Marie-Thérèse and me."

"I—I'll be going back to the U.S.," said Bob.

"Not unless you grow wings," said the mayor. "The proletariat has got the country by the balls. And we intend to make the fat boys in Paris sweat as long as possible. So you see there's nothing to do but drink and talk politics. And we'll do both tomorrow over lunch. *Ciao*, Bobbie. *Bon soir, ma petite*." He kissed Nicole and ambled off.

"Quite a character, eh?" said Nicole to Bob. "Can you imagine what France would be if he replaced de Gaulle?"

"Yes." Bob smiled. "It would be Italy."

She laughed. "You're funny," she said.

"No, I just think I'm a little high. Should I be drinking this wine at all?"

"Don't worry," she replied. "You've got a doctor in attendance."

He took another sip of Louis's *muscat* and then looked inquisitively at Nicole.

"You were just starting to explain why you would never marry."

"I just know I won't." She shrugged.

"But *why?*"

"Maybe I am crazy, but I don't think marriage is for everybody. At least not for me. I enjoy being independent too much. That doesn't necessarily mean being lonely."

"I'm sure," Bob interrupted, "someone as attractive as you—" He stopped himself. He had not wanted to express it in a way that revealed how strongly he was affected by her beauty. He had intended a theoretical conversation between two acquaintances.

"Don't you ever want children?" he asked.

"I've thought of it. I think I will. If I find someone I like enough to make a child with."

"And you'd raise it yourself?"

"Why not?"

"That's pretty . . . avant-garde."

"You mean 'unbourgeois,' don't you? Anyway, I think I'm strong enough to be a parent on my own. And Sète is certainly not bourgeois. Shall we have another drink?"

"Thanks. I've had more than my share."

"Go on—I'm driving."

Not that he was drunk. But in a way he felt himself losing control. He struggled to keep the conversation abstract and innocuous. The congress at Montpellier. P. Herbert Harrison. The book Sheila was editing.

"You must love her very much," said Nicole.

"She's why I believe in marriage," Bob replied.

"I envy you that faith," said Nicole Guérin, her manner for the first time slightly wistful.

They drank coffee. It was getting late. The place was quieting down.

"I should really be getting back," said Bob.

"Yes," she agreed, and stood up. "You're starting to look uncomfortable. It's either fatigue, your bruise—or my personality."

He thought he should protest. But her triply accurate diagnosis was irrefutable.

"Come on," she said. "You'll be in bed in twenty minutes."

The highway was lit only by the moon. She had taken the Route de la Corniche out of Sète, to show him the tranquil shore before returning to Montpellier.

"Tomorrow I'll show you some wild forests and extraordinary limestone formations we call *causses*. They're not quite the Grand Canyon, but they do have a certain savage beauty. Anyway, you'll see."

Will I? thought Bob. Do I have to face temptation again in the light of day? He did not reply, hoping his silence would discourage her from making plans for them.

"Can you see those beaches we're passing?" she asked.

"Yes. They're nice and white."

"And deserted. Doesn't the water look inviting?"

"Yes." He was being polite.

"Then why don't we take a swim?"

"Now?"

"Not to exercise," she said. "That would be too American. I mean just run in the water and get wet."

She turned to smile at him.

He could not answer yes. He did not want to answer no. He simply let her pull the car onto a small dirt road above the long and silent beach.

They got out and walked to the edge of the sea without speaking. Then they stood there.

"Don't worry," she whispered at last. "The water's warm."

And unself-consciously, she slipped off her clothing till it was all in a tiny pile at her feet.

He gazed at her beauty, silhouetted against the sea and sand.

"Come on, Bob," she said. Again softly.

And now he felt strangely awkward, standing there . . . overdressed.

She stood motionless in the moonlight, as he began to remove his shirt, his shoes, his socks, his trousers. Everything.

"Let's go," she said, starting into the sea. He followed her, letting the gentle waves splash over him.

All the time he was in the water, and especially when she splashed him playfully, he wondered what would happen next. And yet he knew. It was inevitable now. He was swimming in a starlit sea, thousands of miles from all his values. He knew very well what would happen. And he wanted it.

She took his hand as they walked out of the water.

They stopped, the ocean still swirling around their ankles.

She put her face very close to his. They kissed.

"Come back to Sète with me, Bob," she whispered, "no strings, just because tonight we both want to be with one another."

And he answered, "Yes."

30

Bob heard footsteps coming toward him. He looked up. It was Dr. Shelton, still dressed in surgical greens.

"Mr. Beckwith . . ."

Bob stood up, his heart pounding.

"Yes?"

"I think we were in time," said Shelton. "We'll know in about twelve hours, but I'm pretty optimistic. I suggest you go home and get a little rest."

"Can I see him?"

"I'm not sure if he's awake."

"I don't care. I just want to see him breathing."

"Go ahead then. But don't be upset. He looks a lot worse than he feels. He's in room 400."

Bob started to run.

He was out of breath when he reached the room. He opened the door as quietly as possible. The little boy was propped up in bed, one tube in his nostril, another in his arm. His eyes were half closed.

"Jean-Claude?" he whispered. The boy turned his head.

"Bob," he said hoarsely, "it hurts when I speak."

"Then I'll talk and you just nod your head."

He walked slowly toward him.

"You're gonna be okay," he said. "You had a burst appendix. They had to operate, but it'll be okay. The doctor told me."

For a minute the boy just looked at him. Then, despite the discomfort, he spoke.

"I'm sorry, Bob, I cause you so much trouble."

"Shh. Don't be silly." He stroked his hair to reassure him. "And stop talking. Just nod your head."

He nodded his head.

"Good. Now go to sleep and I'll see you in a few hours." He squeezed the boy's hand.

Jean-Claude looked at him and tried to smile. "Don't worry. I am not afraid of hospitals."

He drove back slowly, turning the air conditioner full blast on his face to keep him awake. The storm had ended, but there were puddles everywhere. By the time he reached the house, he could feel a hot humid day beginning.

Sheila came onto the porch when she heard the car. They spoke almost simultaneously.

"How is he?" she asked.

"How're the girls?" he asked.

"You talk first," she said.

"It looks pretty good."

"Thank God. We were all so worried."

He looked at his wife. There were a million things he longed to tell her.

"I love you, Sheila," he said. "Do you still believe that?"

"Yes," she answered, almost shyly. And put her arm around him as they walked into the house.

The girls were sitting on the steps in their pajamas.

"How is he?" Paula burst out.

"He'll be okay," said Bob. He sat down wearily.

"This is all my fault," said Jessica. "When you were gone, I was the scaredest I've ever been in my life."

"Me too," said Paula.

"No, girls. It's nobody's fault but mine," said Bob. He wrapped his daughters in his arms and held them tight. He could feel their fright and confusion. "We're gonna be together," he said. "Always. Nothing will ever change that."

He felt a tender touch on the back of his neck.

"You're really exhausted, honey," Sheila said. "You ought to get some sleep."

Yes. He was almost numb. All he could feel was the emanations of their love.

"Go on, Daddy," said Jessica. "Mom's right." He nodded, kissed them both and started up the stairs, with Sheila just behind him.

She helped him off with his clothes and into warm pajamas. He could barely manage a thank you as he crawled under the covers and closed his eyes.

Sheila bent over and kissed his cheek.

"I missed you," she whispered, thinking he was already asleep. But he had heard, and, eyes still shut, reached up his hand, fishing for hers. She grasped it. He brought their enlaced fingers to his lips, hugging them, thinking, Please don't let go, Sheila. Never, never, never.

When he woke some six hours later, she was sitting on the edge of the bed with a cup of hot coffee.

"I've got to call the hospital," he said.

"It's all right," Sheila answered softly. "Dr. Shelton phoned while you were sleeping. He says the signs are good. His pulse is down and his fever is much lower." And then she added, "He's asking for you."

"Oh." And then he said, "Will you come too?"

She thought a moment and then answered, "Yes.

In the next two weeks, while Jean-Claude was gradually regaining strength, Bob and Sheila came to visit every day.

One morning when Bob had business to attend to, Sheila drove to see Jean-Claude on her own. He looked uneasy when he noticed she was by herself.

"I've brought the books you asked for," she smiled, sitting near his bed. "*Histoire Générale, Spider-Man* and *The Incredible Hulk.*"

"You are very kind," he said.

She sensed that he was trying to convey something more.

"I'm very fond of you," she said, to show she understood.

He looked away.

"As soon as I am well I will go back to France," he said, still facing away.

"Of course not. You'll come and stay with us."

He turned and looked at her. His eyes were sad.

"When I came here, I did not know . . . who Bob was."

"Yes, I know."

"But you did?"

Sheila hesitated for a moment, then decided honesty was better than awkward diplomacy. "Yes," she said. "He told me."

"Were you angry with him?"

"Yes."

"Then you must also have been angry with me."

How could she respond to this? She took his hand.

"I suppose I was, at first," she said gently. "But now we know each other. Now we're friends."

He had listened very carefully. She could not tell if he believed her. At last he said:

"You are very kind, Sheila."

Jessica no longer fought with Bob. She who had once been voluble and eloquent was now quiet and withdrawn. She spent a lot of time out of the house. Bob preferred to think it was a stage of adolescence and assumed—at least he hoped—she would get over it. And he made frequent efforts at conciliation.

"Say, Jess, why don't we all go to the flicks tonight? I hear *Silent Movie* is hilarious."

"Sorry, Dad. I've got a previous engagement. A date, actually."

"Oh. Anyone I know?"

"David Ackerman," said Jessie.

"Oh—*Davey*. Oh. Nice boy."

There was only one movie house in the vicinity, a gray barn with ancient wooden seats and walls so thin that you could hear the ocean even during the Westerns. Bob took Paula and Sheila that night, sitting between them, with an arm around each. After the film, as they were buying ice cream cones, he caught sight of Jessica and Davey, walking side by side. Did she notice him? He couldn't tell. Anyway, he thought, I guess I should be pleased she's growing up.

As they were driving home, all three of them squeezed in the front seat of the car, Paula asked, "How much longer will Jean-Claude be in the hospital?"

"Dr. Shelton thinks about another five days," said Sheila.

"What happens then?" she asked uneasily.

"Your mother and I think he should come home and stay with us till he's stronger," Bob said.

"Oh," said Paula. "Have you told Jessie?"

"Yes," said Bob.

"What did she say?"

"Nothing," Sheila answered.

Jean-Claude was pale and thin, but otherwise looked healthy. It was difficult to tell how he felt about the prospect of returning to the Beckwith house. For there, two weeks ago, the nightmare had begun for him. Bob wondered as he drove him if the boy was apprehensive about confronting Jessica and Paula.

Sheila met them at the door and kissed Jean-Claude. They went inside. The house seemed oddly empty.

"Where are the girls?" Bob asked.

"They've been upstairs all morning," Sheila answered, glancing at Bob as if to say, I don't know what's going on. She turned to the boy again. He looked a little tired.

"Why don't you take a nap before lunch, Jean-Claude?"

"Okay."

He began slowly up the stairs and started to his room. When he opened the door he was stunned. Pelé was staring straight at him. That is, a huge life-size poster of the great Brazilian soccer star.

"Do you like it?" asked Paula gaily, jumping from her hiding place.

Before he could respond, Jessie added, "It's personally autographed to you."

He was incredulous. "To me?" He stepped closer and saw inscribed on the soccer ball Pelé was kicking: "To my pal Jean-Claude, Best Wishes, Pelé."

"How did you obtain such a thing?" he asked, his eyes full of wonder.

"My friend's father happens to be his personal lawyer," Jessie answered.

"It's fantastic," the boy exclaimed. "I can't wait to show it to my friend Maurice."

The three children stood there for a moment. Then Paula said:

"We—uh—really missed you."

And Jessie added, "Welcome home."

31

It was nearly the end of July when Jean-Claude arrived home from the hospital. Sheila was due to return to work on the first Monday in August. And Bob grew increasingly uncomfortable at the prospect of having the whole brood on his hands alone. He said nothing to Sheila, but as usual, she did not need words to know what he was thinking.

"Why don't I ask Evelyn for another month's holiday? Even if she says no, she might at least let me drive to Cambridge once or twice a week and bring work back here."

He was touched by her offer. For he knew this might raise hackles at the office.

"But Evelyn's such a stickler. Do you think she'd put up with that kind of arrangement?"

"She'll just have to, Bob. I'll give her an ultimatum."

"Sheila, you're a tiger."

"No I'm not. I'll be quaking when I actually get in the room."

"Then I'll drive you up and be your second."

"What about the kids?"

"We can get someone. Susie Ryder maybe. I'll take care of it. What do you say we go tomorrow?"

"So soon?" she asked, affecting panic.

"I don't want you to get cold feet. Anyway, even if you do, I'll be there to warm them at the last minute."

She smiled at him. He had been living for that look.

"Well?"

He had stood guard on the stone steps outside the Harvard Press, waiting for her to emerge. When she did she was beaming.

"Well," he teased, "in what elevated language did she tell you to go to hell?"

"I'm an idiot, do you know that?" she stated cheerfully. "She said I should have asked her years ago."

"Haven't I always told you you were the best editor they had?"

"Yes, but I didn't believe you."

"Well, this ought to teach you to trust my judgment a little more. Now let's celebrate," he said, taking her hand. "What would you say to a candle-light dinner?"

"It's barely lunchtime."

"We can wait. And meanwhile we'll buy sandwiches and picnic with the college kids along the Charles."

"And what about *our* kids? We've got to get home by a reasonable hour."

"Tomorrow morning's soon enough," he said. "Susie can stay overnight."

She looked at him with a mischievous smile.

"How come you didn't tell me about this arrangement? Are there any other surprises in store?"

"You'll see," he answered. And he felt a surge of joy. Joy born of hope. She hadn't objected to any of his "arrangements." So far anyway.

*　　*　　*

Almost by definition, Harvard Summer School consists of people not otherwise associated with Harvard. Hence as they walked along the riverbank, no one in Cambridge recognized them. They were alone in the summer crowd. They sat down on the grass, ate lunch and watched the many pleasure boats go by.

"If I see Noah's ark," said Bob, "I'll flag it over and we'll volunteer as passengers."

"I somehow think they'd want two younger specimens."

"Like hell. We're young. At least you are. Every undergraduate we've passed today has given you the eye."

"But still, we're not as young as Jessica and Davey."

"What? Come on, Sheila. She's an infant! This Davey nonsense is sheer anti-me rebellion."

"Bob, you'd better face up to the fact that your daughter is a blush away from womanhood."

"Years, Sheila. Years."

She lay back, plucked a blade of grass and began chewing it.

"Not even MIT professors can make time stop," she said.

He looked down at her freckled face.

"I don't want to stop time," he said with emphatic seriousness. "I just want to turn it back."

The candlelight dinner was not at any restaurant. While she was inside confronting Evelyn Unger, he had dashed to Mass Avenue and bought canned vichyssoise, frozen chicken divan, salad in a bag and two bottles of very good champagne. As for the candles, there would be plenty in the house in Lexington.

They sat cross-legged in front of the fire and talked for a long time.

At one point he asked, "Do you remember when we first made love?"

"I try not to. I was so scared."

"And I was so gauche. Do you think your parents ever guessed what we were doing while we house-sat for them?"

"Probably. We both looked so utterly miserable."

They laughed together.

"I don't know why it went so badly, Sheil. I memorized every manual—even the *Kama Sutra*."

"In English?"

"I know it didn't seem that way." He grinned. "But we improved, didn't we?"

"Yes," she said. "Practice makes perfect." She took another sip of champagne.

He moved close to her.

"I've missed our practice sessions," he said quietly.

She did not reply. He moved even closer.

"You know," he whispered, "you're the only woman in the world whose soul is as beautiful as her body."

He realized as he said it that it might sound like a phony line to her. In the past he'd said such things and had been certain that she knew he meant them. Which he had. With all his heart. But now, after everything that had happened, it was possible she'd never trust a word he said.

"I mean it, Sheila," he whispered, brushing back her hair and kissing her forehead.

She did not move away. He took that as a hopeful sign.

"Do you believe I'll always love you?" he asked softly.

She bent her head down. And then answered, "I think so."

He put his arm around her and said firmly, "You *believe* it. Take it as an article of faith. I love you more than life."

Tears began to trickle slowly down her cheeks.

He looked at her and murmured, "I know, I know. I've hurt you so much."

Then both of them were silent. His heart ached for her. He was desperate to make it right again.

"Sheila, could you ever—" He stopped. It was so difficult. "Do you think you might in time be able to forget the way I've hurt you?"

Silence once again. Then she looked up.

"I'll try," she whispered. "I can't promise more, Bob. But I'll try."

He took her in his arms. As she leaned back she spilled her champagne.

"That's good luck," he said, kissing her eyes. Her cheeks. Her lips.

At last she responded, embracing him.

"I've missed you terribly," she said. "I couldn't bear the thought of losing you. Oh, Robert . . ."

He kissed her everywhere, releasing all the tenderness pent up so long. And prayed that someday all the pain he knew that she still felt would disappear.

Please, God. I love her so.

32

"QUICK, JOHNNY, I'M FREE—PASS ME THE BALL!"

In late summer a young man's fancy turns to thoughts of autumn sports. The casual soccer sessions on the Nanuet High School field had gradually become serious scrimmages. But Davey Ackerman and his new friend, "Johnny" Guérin, were still allowed to play with the varsity boys. And they always contrived to be on the same team. Ever since Jean-Claude was well enough to kick a ball again, he and Davey had worked out together, evolving a terrific give-and-go which would always get one of them past the defense into a clear shot at the goal. Their teamwork made Bernie ecstatic and Jessie sullen.

It was the final week of August. Afternoon shadows were growing longer. The Beckwiths and the Ackermans had come to watch the two kids match their skills against the bigger boys.

"What a combo," shouted Bernie as they scored their second goal. He slapped Bob on the back. "Terrific, huh?"

Paula clapped. Jessica sat motionless until her gallant knight waved at her as if to dedicate the goal. She acknowledged with a little wave. Sheila and Nancy were busy discussing books and failed to notice the heroics.

There is a touch of sadness at the close of summer, when the trees begin to hint it will soon end. And despite its tumultuous beginning, the summer was concluding with a certain harmony.

After the game, Bob and Bernie jogged around the track. Jean-Claude and Davey stayed on the field, practicing corner kicks. Sheila offered to drive Nancy and the girls home. Only Paula refused, seemingly determined to keep her father always within view.

"Too bad the kid's gotta go," said Bernie as they chugged around the far curve. "He's got great potential."

"Yeah," said Bob.

"Too bad," repeated Bernie. "In seven years those two coulda made Yale invincible."

"Yeah," said Bob, thinking, Bern, you have the soul of a soccer ball.

Ten minutes later, Bernie summoned the two players with a shout.

"Come on, gang, it's time for chow."

They jogged side by side to the edge of the track.

"Can Johnny eat at our house?" Davey asked.

"May I?" Jean-Claude asked Bob.

"Sure."

"Can he sleep over too, Uncle Bob?"

"If it's okay with Nancy," said Bob.

"She won't mind," said Bernie. "Come on, guys. Let's hit the road."

Paula followed them, a step behind.

Dinner conversation seemed a bit subdued.

"Gosh," said Paula, "it feels funny not having him here."

No one had removed the place mat set for Jean-Claude.

"Well, better start getting used to it," said Jessie to her sister. "He'll be gone for good soon. Won't he be, Dad?"

"Yes," said Bob quietly, "any day now." He said it as matter-of-factly as he could. He wanted Sheila to know he had no qualms.

The girls went to bed about nine-thirty. Bob went upstairs to kiss them good night. Jessica, even while accepting his embrace, let him know she was getting too old for this sort of thing.

When he came back downstairs, Sheila was putting on a sweater.

"Feel like a little walk?" she asked.

"Sure."

Bob got a flashlight and they went out to stroll beneath the trees. It was silent except for the sea behind the house. Peaceful. He felt close to her. He took her hand.

"Bob?"

"Yes?"

"You want him to stay, don't you?"

"Of course not," he said very quickly. "It's out of the question. We agreed—"

"That isn't what I asked. I wanted to know how you feel. Honestly."

They walked for a few steps before he answered.

"Well, I'm not overjoyed at his leaving. But hell, it's a fact of life. I mean"—he hoped this admission wouldn't hurt her—"I do like him a lot."

"We all do," she said softly.

"Yeah," he replied, thinking, This is her way of consoling me.

"I mean me too, Bob."

They had reached a small clearing in the woods.

She stopped and looked at his face, with its forced stoic expression.

"He doesn't have to go, Bob," she said.

Though they were standing very close, he wasn't certain he had actually heard her.

"Look," she continued, "something terrible happened to us. It will take years for the scars to really heal. . . ."

She paused.

"But it has nothing to do with him, Bob. Nothing. Besides, he's your child. Do you think you'd ever forget him if he went away?"

He hesitated.

"No. I guess not."

Then she continued his thoughts for him.

"There would always be a part of you that would be wondering how he was, what had become of him. . . ."

"Yes," he said quietly.

"And he'd be thinking of you."

Bob was silent.

"He adores you. We can all see that."

Bob refused to let himself surrender to the impulse of the moment.

"Honey, the most important thing in my life is you and the girls."

"Yes," she answered. "Let's talk about them for a moment."

They sat down on an ancient tree trunk lying in the darkened forest.

"They're both in pretty fragile shape, I know," he said. "Especially Jessie with that whole not-caring act."

"And Paula?"

"She seems to be taking it better, for some reason."

"Bob, she's so obsessed with losing you she won't

let you out of her sight. Haven't you noticed that every morning, and I mean *every* morning, she peeks into our room and looks at your side of the bed. She's petrified."

Bob took a deep breath. Now, retrospectively, he realized how desperately Paula had been clinging to him.

"But if he did stay . . . ?"

"Bob, we'd have a better chance if he were here instead of somewhere in the corner of everyone's imagination. I mean yours and mine—and especially the girls'. They'd always be afraid that you might go away."

He reflected for a moment.

"Oh, Christ," he said. And thought, I've really put them in a no-win situation.

"There's one more thing," Sheila said gently.

"Yes?"

"You love him."

"Yes," he answered. And thought, Thank you, Sheila.

He broached it the next morning while Jean-Claude was still at Bernie's.

"Jessie and Paula, your mother and I were considering asking Jean-Claude to . . . stay on with us. We'd like to know what you two think."

"Is this true, Mom?" Jessie asked. "It isn't just his idea?"

"I suggested it," said Sheila. For the moment Jessie withheld comment. Bob turned to Paula.

"Gee," she said uneasily. "Would he be in my grade?"

"I suppose so," said Bob. "They'd probably make him take a test. But how would you *feel* about it?"

Paula pondered for another moment. "We start

French this year," she said. "It would be neat to have Jean-Claude around to help."

Which was her way of saying yes.

"Jessie?" Bob inquired.

"I have no objection," she said tonelessly. And then added, "Actually, I like him quite a lot."

Bob looked across at Sheila. They smiled at one another.

Bob drove to Bernie's about noon. The smile on Jean-Claude's face suggested not only that he was happy to see Bob, but that he had heard more than enough of Bernie's pep talks on the future of world sport. Bob asked the boy to take a walk with him along the beach.

"Summer's almost over," Bob said as they surveyed the empty shore.

"I know," the boy replied. "I must be leaving soon."

"That's just what I wanted to talk to you about, Jean-Claude," said Bob. "Uh—how would you feel about staying on with us?"

The boy stopped, a surprised look on his face.

"I mean sort of joining the family," Bob continued.

"That is impossible," said the boy.

"Oh, I know what you're thinking. But everyone is sorry for what happened. All of us want you to stay. Wouldn't you like that?"

Jean-Claude did not know how to answer. At last he spoke. Very shyly.

"Bob, I cannot. School—*la rentrée*—starts in fifteen days."

"But you could go to school here, Jean-Claude. Besides, where would you live in France?"

"At St. Mâlo," the boy replied.

"What's that?"

"A school. It is where my mother wanted me to go when I was eleven. To be with other boys. But Louis has been speaking to the director. He says I can start now if I pass certain examinations. And I have studied hard."

So that explains all his reading.

"But we want you to live with us," said Bob. "We . . . love you."

The boy looked up at him.

"Bob, I must go to St. Mâlo. It is what my mother planned. And it is the right thing."

Bob looked down at his son. Did he understand what he was saying?

"Is that really what you want—to be alone?"

Please change your mind, Jean-Claude.

"Bob, I must go . . . for many reasons."

"Are you positive, Jean-Claude?"

The boy seemed at the limit of his strength.

"Yes," he said softly, and turned his gaze away. Toward the sea.

33

THERE WAS NOTHING MORE TO SAY, REALLY. BOB booked a flight for three days later. The leave-taking was subdued. Sheila and the girls stood on the porch and watched the car go off. No one cried. Yet each had the vague sensation that the others would, eventually.

Bob wanted the ride to Logan to last forever. There was so much he wanted to tell the boy. To clarify his feelings. Establish their relationship. Express his love. And yet they barely spoke during the journey.

He parked the car and took the green valise out of the trunk. Jean-Claude carried his red flight bag and they walked to TWA, where the boy was checked in for flight 810 and the suitcase sent via Paris on to Montpellier. Bob walked him to the gate. It was only six-thirty. They still had some time. The sky outside was not yet dark, although the airport lights were beginning to come on, anticipating nightfall.

The big white 747 was crouched like a friendly elephant, waiting to take on passengers. Since it

was the end of summer, not many people were
flying to Europe. The departure lounge was quiet.
Now and then a flight was called. Not his. Not yet.
The woman calling flights had no emotion in her
voice.

They sat side by side in white plastic chairs.

"Do you have enough to read, Jean-Claude?"

"I have my books."

"Oh, yes, of course. Good luck on the exams. Uh
—are you nervous?"

"A little."

"You'll be sure and let me know how it turns
out?"

"Yes."

"And we'll stay in touch. . . ."

The boy hesitated slightly, then said, "Yes."

"*TWA announces its final call for flight 810, non-
stop 747 service to Paris. Immediate boarding Gate
17.*"

They stood up without a word and started slowly
toward the gangway door. But there was still something important Bob had to say.

"Uh—if you like, you could visit us again next
summer. Or even Christmas. I mean anytime."

"Thank you," he said.

"So maybe you'll come next summer, huh?"

"Maybe."

Or maybe not, thought Bob. Very likely not.

The lady taking tickets seemed to be signaling.

"I should go, Bob," said the little boy.

No, please, thought Bob. Not yet. Not yet.

Now Jean-Claude held out his hand and, as if
preparing for the life awaiting him across the ocean,
spoke his final words in French.

"*Au revoir, Papa.*"

Bob could hold out no longer. He swept the little
boy into his arms and hugged him. He could feel

the boy's chest breathing rapidly against his own. They spoke no words. He longed to say I love you, but was scared of breaking down. So he simply held his son. And hugged him, wanting never to let go.

On the periphery of his awareness, someone said the doors were going to close.

He put the little boy down. And took a final look at him.

"Go on," he whispered hoarsely, unable to say more. His throat was tight.

The boy looked up at him for a split second, and without another word, turned toward the gate.

Bob watched him hand his ticket to the hostess, watched her tear a page off. Watched him walk straight-backed, carrying his flight bag, down the gangway onto the plane. And disappear.

The gate closed.

A few minutes later, the white jumbo slowly backed away, then headed toward the runway into the growing darkness.

Bob stood there for a long while.

At last he turned and started walking slowly down the now deserted corridor.

Maybe I'll meet him some day. But we'll be strangers really. Because I'm gonna miss those times when he most needs me. So he'll have never had a father.

And I'll have never had a son.

ABOUT THE AUTHOR

Born in New York City in 1937, Erich Segal earned his A.B. and Ph.D. at Harvard and then moved to Yale to begin a career as a teacher of Latin and Greek.

During one Christmas vacation, he learned that the young wife of a former student had just died. He was moved to write about it, and the result was the worldwide phenomenon *Love Story*. The sequel, *Oliver's Story*, was also a bestseller, but it was only with this third novel, *Man, Woman and Child*, that critical acclaim was added to popular success.

A veteran of more than forty marathon races, Erich Segal has been a television commentator for three Olympic games.

He lives and teaches in New England, the setting of his first three novels and of the fourth, on which he is currently at work.

He is married and has one child.